Restoring ASHFORD MANOR

EARLS OF
ENGLAND
· BOOK THREE ·

Restoring ASHFORD MANOR

ANGELA JOHNSON

SWEETWATER BOOKS

An imprint of Cedar Fort, Inc. • Springville, Utah

ISBN 13: 978-1-4621-4319-1

Published by Sweetwater Books, an imprint of Cedar Fort, Inc.
2373 W. 700 S., Springville, UT 84663
Distributed by Cedar Fort, Inc., www.cedarfort.com

Library of Congress Control Number: 2022937824

Cover design by Shawnda T. Craig
Cover design © 2022 Cedar Fort, Inc.
Edited by Evelyn Nichols

Printed in the United States of America

10 9 8 7 6 5 4 3 2 1

Printed on acid-free paper

For Joslynn . . . You're done!

Additional Books by Angela Johnson

Earls of England Series
The Earl of Arundel
Saved by Scandal

An Assignation to Remember Series
Wit & Intrigue
Unmasking a Lady
Maid in the Stars

Fernley Family: A Regency-Era Romance
Earl Grafton and the Traitor

One

Lucas Grantham, the Earl of Branton, stood outside the home he'd known most his life looking into the windows he knew belonged to the morning room, dreading the moment he would have to enter. In his mind he could see the perfectly placed furniture, the blue cushions, and expensive tapestries ready for morning visits. He hoped he would be his parents' sole visitor of the day. They had much to discuss.

Gathering his courage, Lucas stopped dawdling and stepped up to the door and knocked before he lost his nerve. The conversation he planned to have with his parents wouldn't be easy.

"Lord Branton, we were not expecting you today." Mr. Mason was the first obstacle to meeting with his parents and he was well trained. "If you leave your card, I will send for you when Duke and Duchess Wymount are home to visitors."

"My parents are always home at this hour, unless the duchess is out for visits, but I happen to know she has not left Lydney Hall in the early hours for many years." Stepping past Mason, Branton threw his hat on the table in the entryway followed by his gloves and greatcoat. He wasn't in the mood to argue with Mason. "You will let them know I am in the morning room."

"My lord, the morning room is not ready for visitors."

Lucas ignored the butler and walked to the doors he knew led to the blue pastel room. As he opened the door, he was disappointed to see the furniture draped with large white cloths and the walls in a state of disrepair. "What is happening here?"

"I have grown weary of the blue." Duchess Wymount gracefully glided down the stairs an air of superiority in her upturned nose.

"The blue was perfectly fine, your grace."

"Do not speak to me with such insolence. What are you doing here?"

The lack of affection from his mother wasn't a surprise, but even after years of neglect it still stung. Searching for the courage he'd carried with him to the front door, Lucas straightened his shoulders and faced his mother. "I need to speak with you and Father."

The duchess waved her hand in a shooing motion. "We are not prepared for an audience today. You may come back next week."

Lucas was past caring what anyone thought of him, and so it didn't matter that Mason stood with his hat, coat, and gloves ready to escort him out of the house. Lucas had a purpose in coming to Lydney Hall, and he wouldn't leave without speaking to his parents. "By next week we could find ourselves the newest tenants in debtor's prison. It is best you clear your calendar for the day."

"Such dramatics are unbecoming of a young man in your situation. I am certain Wymount has our finances under control." The duchess passed by him without pausing and made her way to the dining room. Lucas followed. He had no intention of sitting down to eat, but he needed his mother to hear him out.

Did she truly trust Wymount? Lucas didn't. His father had not only neglected his children, but he'd also allowed the estate finances to fall into ruin. There were very few options, one of which required his parents to retrench in one of the country estates. They needed to close the London house and live on a budget.

As he entered the dining room, he was dismayed to find a large spread of breakfast foods on the sideboard. Most of it would go to waste. "Wymount has done nothing to correct the estate finances. I worry it will not be long before we are in severe trouble."

He was underplaying the severity of their situation. As the duchess placed three strawberries and two slices of bread on her plate, Lucas closed his eyes to calm down. Would she truly eat so little when there was so much?

"I have seen no evidence of what you claim. You are crying wolf."

"No, your grace, I am not making up stories." Knowing he wouldn't get anywhere with his mother, Lucas turned from the room to approach the duke. Wymount would have to listen to him. "Where is his grace?"

Mason stood in the same position, Lucas's outerwear still in hand. "He has not left his chambers, my lord."

This wasn't a surprise. Their family physician had diagnosed Duke Wymount with a severe case of melancholy years before. It was the duke's responsibility to see after the estates, the finances, and the title. This included his family, but the duke had fallen short of his duty to all things important. Instead, he spent his days doing absolutely nothing in a dark bedchamber.

Charging up the marble staircase, and down the over decorated hallway leading to the chambers he knew to be his father's, Lucas ignored the warnings of the duchess and the butler to leave Wymount alone. They would lose everything if a solution was not found. He had to stop the excessive spending on clothing, trips to the continent, hats, and the needless redecorating of Lydney Hall.

The current duke and duchess had spent Lucas's entire inheritance. He would have nothing to care for the land and title, let alone living expenses before long. Pounding on his father's bedchamber door, Lucas stood back and waited for an answer, but he received silence. He knew it would be very improper to enter without approval, but he was finished waiting for his parents to wake up and pay attention to him.

Lucas opened the door and entered the musty dark bedchamber. With the light from the corridor, he crossed to a window and threw open the drapes. He would speak with the duke even if he had to endure his father lying in a bed.

"What the deuce are you doing?" Wymount growled as he pulled his bedcovers over his head.

"We need to speak, your grace."

"Later. I am not well. I am very ill."

"I will call for a physician, if that is the case." Lucas didn't have money to spare for a physician. He truly hoped the duke wasn't ill.

"Go away. The light causes my chest to ache."

The light? Lucas nearly burst out laughing over his father's claim, but it was best not to anger the duke more than he already had. "Your grace, we need to speak about the estate finances. They are an absolute mess, and we cannot continue on in this frivolous manner of spending."

Wymount threw his bedcovers to the side and crawled out of bed. Glaring at Lucas, he moved to a chair and pulled a lap blanket over his thin frail legs. "I am aware of our situation. There is nothing we can do about it."

"Nothing?" Lucas threw himself into the only other chair in the room. "You and the duchess can retrench and live frugally in the country. My sisters do not need to be at finishing school. You could employ a governess for a fourth of the cost you spend now on their living expenses and education. With these changes, a new crop rotation, and wise investments, we can correct the damage within seven years."

Wymount shook his head. "I have already tried. I do not have the energy to do so again."

"I respectfully disagree with you. You have not tried. You have spent the last decade in your bedchamber hiding from life. You allowed this to happen."

Wymount stood, his bedclothes hung from his malnourished body, his white legs dangerously thin came into full view as the blanket fell to the ground. "Do not be cheeky with me, boy. You may be my heir, but you do not have the right to speak to me with such insolence."

Rightfully chastened, Lucas took a moment to calm his racing heart. Wymount was the duke, he held the higher rank, but he wasn't behaving as the owner of the title should. Everything Lucas had learned about leading a duchy and caring for the estates was in contradiction to how Wymount handled the job.

"Your grace, I meant no disrespect, but can you not agree to work with me on the situation? Closing Lydney Hall will stop the constant need for the duchess to replenish her wardrobe with the latest fashions, there will be fewer parties to attend in the country, and if the girls are home with you and mother, it will not take long for other expenses to right themselves.

Lucas knew these few things wouldn't solve all their problems, but it was a start. They could take the extra funds and ask their solicitor to make solid investments, which would yield profit over time.

Wymount sat back in his chair and placed his hand over his chest. "You are an insolent fool. Do you truly believe I have not tried to stop the excessive spending? The duchess is miserable without her entertainment. I refuse to take it away from her."

He knew this wouldn't be an easy conversation, but the lack of help from his father was disappointing. He'd hoped they could form an alliance and stop the financial blood bath, but instead, his father had known everything about their financial situation and had allowed it to continue. Knowing he would get no further and resolve nothing, Lucas stood, bowed, and moved toward the exit.

"Close the drapes," Wymount moaned as he moved back to his bed.

Lucas thought about leaving without doing his father's bidding, but it would only prove to be a juvenile act. He crossed the bedchamber again, closed the curtains, and then left his father to his misery. Standing at the top of the stairs, Lucas wasn't surprised to find Mason standing in the same spot holding his coat, hat, and gloves. It was time for Lucas to leave.

"If you send your card at least a week in advance, I can prepare the duke and duchess for a visit." Mason was a loyal servant, and after the interactions he'd just experienced, Lucas couldn't fault him for the admonishment.

"Thank you, Mason. I will try to remember." As he walked away from Lydney Hall he vowed he would never go back. The brisk autumn air did nothing to calm his nerves. The bustling streets of London served only to heighten his frustrations, and he vowed once he took his father's title of Duke Wymount, he would hire a steward to care for the property instead of doing so himself. With the house located in London, he would prefer to skip the season or rent rooms for the rest of his days, if only it meant he didn't have to step foot in Lydney Hall again.

All he'd ever wanted from his father and mother was a sign of affection. The apathetic lack of attention from the duke and the neglect of the duchess stung more than he cared to admit. When they looked down upon him from their lofty station, he squirmed like a schoolboy ready to take a whipping. He'd wanted to make them proud and hoped they would find it within their hearts to care for him, but they never had. Even with everything he'd accomplished as a person, a member of Society, and their son, they'd pushed him away.

Pulling his coat tight around his body to keep the cool air away, he entertained the notion of abandoning his family forever. There were times when a title skipped a generation, if there wasn't an heir who took up the mantle. He entertained a life on the continent away from family responsibilities and his parents and imagined the freedom such a life would bring, but that was all it ever amounted to, imagination. He'd been raised to take the mantle of duke, and he would fulfill his duties as expected.

His five sisters had been sent away to school before he'd returned from his time at Oxford, and therefore he didn't know them. Once he'd realized his parents cared for only themselves, he'd vowed to keep his distance. Until he'd discovered the financial discrepancies. Without the funds to pay for his rented rooms and servants, he would have to live at Lydney Hall or find a profession. Working wasn't an option. An earl with a profession would be ousted from what was considered respectable Society. Gathering his courage to confront the duke and duchess had taken weeks. He shouldn't have delayed the confrontation. Each day had taken another toll on the family coffers.

In truth, he'd hoped there was a simple mathematical error within the books. Lucas had poured over each book until his eyes blurred and his head hurt. There was nothing wrong with the mathematics and now he could fully blame his father and mother for all the financial issues they faced.

Lucas knew it wouldn't be long before he would no longer have his rented rooms. His purse had tightened, and the funds would soon be gone and replenished with even less. It was far past time for him to take charge of the financial portion of his father's estates. Although he didn't hold the title of duke, he would find a way to have his father declared incompetent to save the legacy of Wymount. It wasn't his best plan, but if Wymount refused to work on solutions, it left Lucas no choice.

Taking control of the estate finances would be the difference between bringing the entailed estates back to working order or finding themselves in debtor's prison. Lucas would need to speak with his solicitor to start the paperwork. He would have to ask Parliament for an audience, and he would have his father declared incompetent. It pained him to embarrass his father before men who once had considered Wymount their friend, but his father's retreat from Society had left the connections weak.

A claim of incompetence would not go unnoticed amongst the *ton*, but neither would a hoard of debt collectors breaking down the door to take every item that would fetch a price. The keen eyes of every parlor in St. James's Square would be focused upon Lydney Hall if that time came, and Lucas vowed to avoid it at all costs. A smile spread across his face as he considered saving his family from debt, and then it turned upside down into a disappointed frown as he knew it would proclaim him a traitorous son forever more.

If he had the duke declared incompetent, it would destroy the man. Lucas didn't have a lot of peaceful feelings toward his parents, but he didn't want to injure them. Somewhere deep down in his soul he still longed for their praise and care. "There is something seriously wrong with such a hope." He said the words out loud, but only because he wanted to ponder the situation. His parents had left him and his sisters to the care of servants and teachers. They would never be proud of him.

As he entered his rented rooms, Lucas threw his hat and gloves at his valet. "I am leaving for Wymount House within the hour. Please send to the stables to ready my horse."

Instead of staying in town feeling helpless to resolve the increasing debt, he would ride out to Wymount House and start building his defense against the duke. There had to be some way for him to save his ungrateful parents from ruin. But moreover, this was his future, and he wanted a strong legacy. One he could be proud to pass to a future heir.

Two

It was rare for a woman in her fourth season to be asked to dance, for every dance, especially at Almack's, but somehow Lady Marianne Watson defied the rules. From the moment she'd entered Almack's, there hadn't been time for rest. As Mr. Kendall escorted her back to her mother and sisters, Marianne wished there was a chair available. But, at a party as overcrowded as this, only women in sensitive conditions were given seats, which included her sisters and her mother.

Marianne thanked Mr. Kendall and let out a sigh of relief as he walked away. He was kind, but she wished she could sit and massage her feet before the next dance. Charlotte tried to make room for her to share a chair, but with Charlotte's expanding waist, there was no room. She and Lord Haughton arrived from Scotland to surprise everyone on the upcoming birth of their child. She had some months left, but was larger than Anne, who was also expecting.

"There is not enough room," Marianne said voice tinged with regret. She would never ask her sisters to make space in their conditions and the silk muslin of her light blue dress would never survive sitting. The wrinkles would put an end to any man asking for a dance and she hoped Mr. King would ask her to stand up with him one more time that night.

"I am sorry, Marianne, your feet must be in pain." Charlotte winced in compassion as she looked down.

"I have nothing to complain about," Marianne said with a sassy large smile. "It is not every evening at Almack's where a woman who is almost on the shelf is asked to dance with such vigor."

"You are too hard on yourself," her mother said with a disapproving frown, "you are nowhere near being on a shelf. If your father hears such a statement, he will find you a match, so you must stay silent."

Marianne groaned, along with her sisters. Their father's idea of matches never ended well. First there was Lady Olivia for Phillip and then Lord Riley for Charlotte, neither relationship worked and thankfully both ended before either began. "I will do everything I can to find a match before such an eventuality."

Marianne turned as she saw Mr. King in the corner of her eye. He'd already danced with her for the minuet, but there was the chance that he would ask for another dance. Two dances in one night were acceptable. They'd courted for over a month, but he had yet to offer marriage. She hoped he would speak with Ashby soon. Mr. King might not have a title, but his wealth was extensive. Ashby couldn't deny a man of King's worth.

As he drew near, Marianne turned back to her mother. "Are my cheeks pink? Do I look overheated or delighted to be at the ball?"

"You are a picture of beauty, my dear. There is no need for concern."

Looking to Charlotte, Marianne whispered. "How close is he?"

"Nearly upon us. Stay calm."

Marianne's heart pounded in her ears as she waited for the moment Mr. King would ask for a second dance. Turning to meet Mr. King with a smile as he made his final approach, Marianne hoped her blush was truly as magnificent as her mother claimed.

"Lady Marianne, would you dance the next reel with me?" Mr. King's soft voice made her arms tingle with joy. If she could convince him to speak with Ashby, a match would be secured. She'd finally be engaged and would no longer be a burden on her parents.

"I would be delighted." Marianne thankfully kept her voice calm and stepped gracefully toward him as he tucked her arm in the crook of his elbow.

Their courtship had been wonderful. She'd enjoyed every moment with him and hoped he was honestly happy to be with her. There'd been whispers amongst her friends that Mr. Andrew King was a fortune hunter, but she was certain it wasn't true. His pocketbook didn't need her dowry. If he declared himself, she would accept without hesitation.

"Did you see Mr. Widdles trip during the last set?" King asked as the music started and the first steps of the dance began. The twinkle in his eyes told her he was aching for amusement.

"I admit I did not." Marianne tried to ignore this side of Mr. King. Everything about him was wonderful, until he mocked other members of the *ton*.

"A pity. He nearly fell. With his oversized nose throwing him off balance, it would have been a sight."

Thinking back to her previous commitment to accepting an offer from King, Marianne had to admit this was a major flaw in his character. She was not partial to the way he laughed at the misfortune of others and hoped to change this about him once they were married. Marianne had a tender heart, and she truly wished the best for everyone. "I hope he was not injured."

"Marianne, why do you take such pains to speak for the people who I enjoy teasing? Mr. Widdles is a fop, and he deserves to be laughed at."

"I try to put myself in the other person's position, and I would not like it if people were speaking ill of me."

"No one would say anything unfavorable about you. Your reputation is impeccable."

The pleasure pulsating in her chest sent a blush up through her throat and into her cheeks. "Thank you for the kind words."

"They are true. This is the reason I must end our courtship."

Marianne stumbled in her footwork. Reels took most of her concentration. His abrupt statement threw her out of step, and she struggled to find her footing. "End our courtship?" Confused, Marianne moved away from the other dancers. She wanted to know his reasons for ending their arrangement, without the possibility of an eavesdropper. She made her way to a secluded corner and waited for Mr. King to push through the crowed. When he arrived, she hoped he would admit it was a ruse before a proposal.

"Marianne, we have courted for some time, and I believe I know you well enough to determine we will not suit."

She was a fool. During the last month, she'd fully convinced herself she was in love with Mr. King. She thought of him each night before going to sleep and imagined a home and future children. All her boys would have his blond hair and blue eyes. Her girls would also have blond hair. She didn't want any of them to inherit the mess of auburn she'd been cursed with.

"You do not care for me?"

Mr. King shook his head. It was cruel the unfeeling way he broke her heart without a hint of regret upon his face. "You do not care for my humor. Right now, you tolerate the laughter I find when someone slips and falls or when a lady's dress snags on the fire grate. In a year or possibly two, my humor will turn all positive feelings you have for me away."

Marianne hated begging, but she was in love with him. Out of all the men she had danced with and spent time with, he was one man she could see in her future. "Can you not change?"

"No, love. I do not want to change. I am happy with my personality."

Tears sprang to her eyes and Marianne turned away. She didn't want him to see her display of emotion. A gentleman wouldn't have ended a courtship in the middle of a ball. She wanted to be angry with him for making her look the fool; instead, every part of her soul wanted to claim she would always love him no matter his poor choice in humor.

"I will take you back to your family."

Marianne shook her head. "I think not, Mr. King. I would prefer you leave me alone."

"Do not be unreasonable. Everyone will talk if I leave you in the corner."

"You should have considered this before breaking my heart at Almack's. Could you not have called upon me in the morning to speak privately?" Marianne's anger had flared. His choice to converse on this subject at a party was unacceptable. Marianne moved to walk away but stopped as Mr. Brockhurst arrived. She wasn't fond of Brockhurst, but the reminder of accepting the waltz with him was welcome given her current situation.

"Lady Marianne," Mr. Brockhurst said, "I do believe the next set is mine."

Holding back a sigh, Marianne gave her most regal smile and put her hand on his arm. "Yes, Mr. Brockhurst. I do recall you requested the waltz."

If there were any of her suitors she'd prefer to dance a waltz with, it was not Brockhurst. The man was far too old for her. It was rumored he was in his forties. For a woman of two and twenty, it was possible for him to be her father. It was acceptable, in Society for parents to wed their daughters to older men, but Marianne didn't want an old man. She wanted someone young. She wanted what her brothers and sister had found. Marianne wanted love. Mr. King had destroyed everything she'd hoped for, and she would now have to begin anew.

Mr. Brockhurst pulled her close and led her throughout the room in a very uncomfortable dance. He treated her with respect, which was nice, but she wasn't the only available woman amongst the *ton*. He set her nerves on end and worry or an emotion closer to fear nudged her heart. She didn't want his admiration or affections, nor did she want it to appear they were anything more than acquaintances. The evening was turning out to be terrible.

Not knowing how to speak to the man, she stayed silent. When he gave her a smoldering look, she chose to look over her shoulder to the other dancers. She didn't want anyone spreading gossip about their dance or start conjecture surrounding an engagement. Fighting off rumors was useless. Only a well-placed scandal could combat the type of rumors Mr. Brockhurst wanted whispered about the *ton*.

As the dance ended, Marianne let out a sigh of relief, only to cringe at his next request.

"Lady Marianne, it is warm in here. Would you accompany me into a less crowded area?"

Giving her most gracious smile, she responded, "I am not over-heated, sir, if you will return me to my family before you go, I will be thankful."

It was not only his age she opposed. There was also something in his eyes that bothered her. He looked at her as if he were eating a delicious meal. Similar to what she expected in the expression of a ravenous wolf as he stalked his prey.

"Please, Marianne." He leaned low and whispered close to her ear. His breath, a mixture of digested turnips and venison, assaulted her senses. Gasping for air free of his stench, Marianne moved away. She'd never given him leave to refer to her so informally, and the sound of her name on his tongue made her pray she never heard him speak it again. He was a despicable man.

"Sir, you do not have my permission to address me so informally."

"I apologize. I do hope to speak with you in private though. I have a very particular question I would like to ask."

Knowing exactly what he wanted — marriage — Marianne decided it was time to let the man down easily. It was one of the curses of being wealthy. But she knew without question her father would oppose the match if she didn't already feel so inclined. Her father would refuse him based on his lack of title, connections, situation, and money. Acquiescing to his request, Marianne allowed him to lead her to a more secluded area of Almack's. She didn't like the man but injuring his feelings in front of others was uncouth. She'd just been the victim of Mr. King's poor manners; she wouldn't put such a burden upon another.

"Mr. Brockhurst." Marianne began hoping to stop him from making a fool of himself. "It is the start of the season, and I have no intention of becoming engaged so soon." She used her firm yet privileged tone to make him stop in the request.

Shocked by her bold announcement, Mr. Brockhurst reared back his bushy grey eyebrows furrowed in resentment. "You will regret this, Marianne."

"I do not believe I will, Mr. Brockhurst." She moved away as he sneered down at her in a most uncomfortable manner. A cold chill spread through her body agitating her nerves. "If you will excuse me, I find it to be a bit chilly tonight and my family awaits my return."

Her legs wobbled as she pushed around the crowds of jolly conversations. No one in all Almack's was aware of the fear coursing through her body as she remembered the indignation of her refusal to Brockhurst and the disappointment in Mr. King. Her night was ruined.

She wished she could be angry at both men, but the overwhelming emotion boiling inside her stomach was fear. Would her father find her a match, now her chances with Mr. King were over? Would Mr. Brockhurst follow through with his threat for her refusal?

Mr. Brockhurst could be dealt with. She would inform her father of his continued attentions, and hope Ashby would sort the situation. As a rule, she was a very kind person. She loved her family and her friends, but when certain men did not understand she had no interest in them whatsoever, and constantly pursued her, it wore on her nerves. Her dowry was enough to save the misguided investments of many families amongst the *ton*. But she would prefer those struggling financially to move to the country and retrench instead of preying upon wealthy women.

As for Mr. King, she knew that disappointment would likely ruin the entire season. She'd placed so many hopes on a match with him, even if he did have a cruel sense of humor. With her season starting out so poorly, she was certain there would be no way to salvage another year in London.

Rejoining her mother and sisters, she decided it was time to leave. She'd fulfilled all the dance requests made of her and had no desire to dance until the next party, that was if her heart had healed by then. Mr. King had destroyed her confidence. "I have a headache."

Charlotte gave a sympathetic smile, "Brockhurst proposed?"

"I did not give him the opportunity," Marianne said, in the adopted tone of privilege. "I refused him before the question was out. Why do I have to go through this every season? Can men like Brockhurst not find women their own age?" She purposefully kept her disappointment with King silent. It could wait until she was home, for tears would certainly arrive upon speaking the words.

"Quiet Marianne, you do not want to make a scene at Almack's. We will not be invited back." Her mother's stern words told her not to argue. "We will discuss this when we get home."

Anne sat forward. "I am worn out." She looked exhausted, but Marianne was not about to tell her so. "I would like to leave as well."

"So would I," Charlotte said trying to move to her feet.

"I will have a footman find your husbands and prepare our carriage," Marianne responded before either woman could stand. It would not do for her sisters to stand out in the hall waiting for their husbands in the condition they posed. Having a purpose put her immediate worries to the back of her mind.

"Marianne," Phillip said as they rode toward the estate close to London. It hadn't surprised her that Phillip and Emma chose to leave Almack's with the rest of the family. Usually when in town for the season, their family stayed at one of the townhomes, Lancaster House or Norfolk House. But for some reason unbeknownst to all of them, Ashby hired the homes to be renovated and so they were forced to stay at Watson Manor, which was only a short distance from town. It happened to be more comfortable than the townhomes but made for fewer morning visitors, which was one of the more enjoyable parts of the season.

"Hmmm?" Marianne asked, turning from the window. Her thoughts were firmly upon Mr. King's dismissal of their courtship.

"Are you ready to accept any of the men vying for your attentions this season? Mother said you refused Brockhurst. Has Mr. King decided to ask for your hand?"

"Brockhurst is a vile man!" Marianne said without reserve. "Did you expect me to accept him?"

Phillip put his hands up to stop her from continuing. "No, and if you had I would ask if you had punch from the tainted bowl. What about King?"

Letting her anger die out, Marianne understood his question. She shouldn't have jumped to conclusions as he wasn't trying to goad her into the arrangement. "Mr. King and I are no longer courting."

The intake of breath from everyone in the carriage forced the tears she'd held back to the surface. The feigned headache rose into her temples and Marianne was near to drowning in sorrow. They wouldn't press her, not now as her voice faltered and she bit back a sob. Phillip's arm went around her as he pulled her into his side for an embrace.

"I am sorry to hear this. I thought King was a better man than that."

She wanted to defend Mr. King, but he'd treated her poorly. She hadn't deserved his abrupt dismissal. She wanted love, and one day she might agree with Mr. King's assessment of the situation, but for now her heart ached. Her siblings were the picture of happiness. Much happier than her parents ever had been, which was enviable. Phillip always found a reason to hold Emma's hand in the carriage or to be close to her when out in Society. Haughton might not be as publicly adoring as Phillip, but she could see Haughton loved Charlotte all the same.

Allowing her tears to fall and the emotion to show in her voice, Marianne needed her brother and sister to know they'd found matches others could only dream of finding. "I want what you have with Emma, and what Charlotte has with Haughton."

Haughton cleared his throat. "How many times do I have to ask you to call me Garrett?"

Pulling out of self-pity, Marianne attempted to tease her new brother. Laughter could help her hold in the ugly sobs she hoped would wait for her bedchamber. "I do not know, my lord, but perhaps once I know you a little better. You did whisk my sister off to Scotland for almost a year before bringing her back to me. I do not know if I can ever forgive you. Wedding tours are not usually so extensive."

"Marianne," Charlotte said with a laugh, "we were only gone seven months."

"And you have come back completely changed." Marianne motioned toward her sister's expanding belly. "I cannot accept you this way as I did not see the beginning of the changes. Also, you are enormous."

She was teasing her sister and brother-in-law, which made everyone smile. Until Charlotte wiped a tear away. Immediately chastened, Marianne took hold of her sister's hand. "I apologize, Lottie, I did not mean it to be harsh."

"Oh, it is not your words." She sniffed into her husband's handkerchief. "I had Lady Violet make a vile comment to me this evening. Since I am so large, everyone thinks I was ruined before we were married."

Phillip and Haughton both gave cries of outrage. Marianne didn't admit to hearing the gossip. But if anyone knew the situation behind Haughton's and Lottie's marriage, they would know the rumors were all conjecture and lies. Marianne saw the glint in Phillip's eyes and knew she must apologize to Lottie and make amends for the words she'd spoken.

"Lottie, I will get the *ton* discussing another topic so they will leave you and my future niece alone."

"Oh, no. I do not think Ashby can handle another scandal from his children. He might do something drastic if you attempt it."

"I will not cause a scandal, I promise."

"Niece?" Haughton said, with his eyebrows quirked, "I rather thought I was getting an heir."

"No, Haughton," Marianne said with mirth, "I will have a niece from one of my sisters. Ashby demands Emma and Phillip produce an heir, so that leaves Lottie and Anne for the niece. If I can have two nieces, then it will be better for me." Musing just a tad more she said, "I must have girls to dote over when I am the spinster aunt."

She shouldn't have included Emma and Phillip in her discussion of children. It was true Ashby demanded an heir, but Emma wasn't increasing. It was a source of contention for the entire family. Marianne was thankful when Phillip brushed her comment aside.

"Which brings us back to my original question, dear sister, for whom do you plan to set your cap?" Phillip asked without any humor.

"Do I have to decide tonight?" Although her heart was still broken, thinking about her future and hoping for a new plan was exactly what she needed. She was thankful Phillip wasn't allowing her to dwell in self-pity.

"Yes, Ashby grows weary. Now Mr. King is no longer an option, there must be another man you have thought of. If tonight were the only chance you had to make a choice, you would choose…?" He let his words trail off in expectation of her ability to finish the sentence.

"I think very highly of a few different men. I know what you are all thinking, how scandalous! But I assure you, they are all well-bred."

She didn't get to see or hear the surprise from her statement as the horses came to a stop and a man yelled out. "Stand and deliver."

"What?" Phillip and Haughton said in unison.

Phillip looked to his wife, "Please stay in here." He moved to open the door but was pushed back by the intruder.

Marianne couldn't say what happened inside the carriage after she was pulled by her arm through the door, but Phillip and Haughton followed her out into the night. The tight grip left her arm tender beneath the increasing pinch of the masked man's fingers.

"You may take our money, sir, but you may not have my sister." Phillip said, his eyes focused in a distrustful glare.

"Keep your money, Arundel, I do not want it. I have what I came for."

Marianne's blood went cold as she recognized the slurred voice. His presence at Almack's had been intolerable. As a man who'd obviously imbibed before undertaking this abduction, he was thoroughly unwanted. "Brockhurst?"

"Unhand my sister and we can discuss this situation as gentlemen." Phillip stood his ground next to Marianne holding her other arm trying to protect her. Although he held tightly, she didn't experience any pain from his contact. She prayed he wouldn't let go.

Pointing a revolver, Brockhurst laughed. "Let go of your sister or you will find I know how to use a weapon."

Marianne screamed. She'd never had a weapon so close to her body. Her vision blurred as she fought to stay present in the moment. If she could break free of his clutches, the weapon would mean nothing.

"You do not frighten me. If you would like to discuss a marriage arrangement, you can come by Watson Manor in the morning. This is not the way to offer for a woman."

"Society be hanged with all of their rules for propriety. This is my offer."

"Then I must refuse you, for I will not have my sister forced into a marriage against her will."

"I did not think you would approve." Brockhurst turned the weapon toward Marianne, and she again cried out. Frightened as she was, she could see the prospect of her death was worse for Phillip. His eyes went wide and his hands lifted in the air. He'd released her arm, which allowed Brockhurst to pull her away.

"Do not harm her."

"Get back in the carriage and I will not have to hurt my Marianne." Brockhurst pulled her toward his horse. He leaned down to whisper in her ear. The reminder of his foul breath pierced her fears. "This is for your refusal of my offer."

He hadn't needed to say the word she'd known why he was holding her captive, but it didn't make it any easier. Forcing her onto his horse, she heard the fabric of her dress rip. When she'd told Charlotte she would find a way to get the old hags of Society gossiping about something else, this situation was nowhere in her thoughts, yet this would certainly fulfil such a promise.

Marianne swayed to the side, her eyes closing as a ringing pierced her ears. She didn't want to lose consciousness, but her mind was having trouble focusing on anything but the ringing and stars. She could see stars, and then there was nothing.

Three

Swooning in frightening situations should be outlawed, Marianne decided as she opened her eyes to find her head was resting upon her captor's shoulder and she was straddling a horse. She'd never ridden a horse without a side saddle, the discomfort of her dress flapping against her bare legs was nothing to Brockhurst's embrace; Brockhurst held her tightly against his body. She wanted to fight and try to get away, but she was pinned and unable to move. The night air smelled of body odors and digested food, making her stomach churn. Turning her head away from the offending smells brought awareness to her captor of her conscious state.

"Do not try to move. I will kill you if you attempt to escape."

"Is this a promise?" Generally, she didn't have a desire to die, and she enjoyed life to the fullest, but a life with Brockhurst would be miserable. She had no intention of marrying the man and she would not endure the scandal this night offered. "Where are you taking me?"

"Gretna Green. It is where all young lovers discover their fates."

"There is only one problem, sir, I am not in love with you." Marianne hadn't planned to attempt escape, but as Brockhurst's hold loosened around her waist she pushed her elbow with force into his gut. The liquid and food from his night at Almack's instantly burst from his mouth. She was thankful he turned to the side, avoiding her dress and hair.

"Useless woman." Brockhurst's growl caused Marianne's gut to clench. Shaking, she tried to focus on anything other than the offending smell of vomit and her abduction. The entire situation would result in an impromptu marriage. Marianne was certain her father wouldn't allow a daughter with a ruined reputation to stay at Wentworth Hall or Watson Manor. Tears trickled out of the corners of her eyes as she considered her options. She had only one choice; she would fight Brockhurst and if she lived through the ordeal she would find her way to Arundel Keep. Phillip would protect her against Ashby. He would allow her to stay at his home and keep her safe.

"We will have to stop for the night." Brockhurst's words sent unpleasant chills through her body. She wouldn't stay at a coaching inn with the man.

"If you try to escape, or tell anyone of the situation, you will find yourself in a severe amount of regret."

She knew his threats held ground. He'd threatened her at the party when she'd refused his offer. As the horse below her continued in a steady pace to their lodging, she knew the result of allowing this man to claim her as a wife would be far worse than any punishment he would present. Straightening her back, she sat tall with determination. She wasn't a little girl who would do as she was told. She was a woman. The daughter of a duke. She would allow this cruel man to kill her if he desired, but she would not marry him.

"Spending a night with me in the coaching inn will solidify our attachment. As soon as we are married, I will let Ashby know of the amount I expect for your dowry and I would like the estate in Ipswich. The research I have done indicates it is outside of the entailment. It should fit my needs well." Brockhurst spoke in a business-like tone as though this was the natural progression of an engagement.

"My father will not give you my dowry or any lands. He made it most plain to both Lottie and I that a ruined woman inherits nothing. Also, it was Phillip's influence and desire for Lord and Lady Haughton to inherit the land in Scotland. Ashby was content with only providing money."

Brockhurst growled. "Then you will have to plead with your brother for his charity, as I have no intention of returning you to your family unscathed."

With his words and the force of his stench, Marianne attempted to move away from his body, but found there was no place to go on the horse. She was stuck until they stopped for the night. Regaining her composure, Marianne scathingly responded with the hope she held in her heart. They wouldn't allow her to be ruined. Not Phillip and Edward. Even now she knew her brothers would be in pursuit. She only hoped there wouldn't be a duel. Brockhurst was rumored to be a talented marksman.

"My family will come for me."

After saying the words and hearing his sinister laugh, she started doubting herself. What had he done to Phillip, Haughton, Emma, and Lottie? Were they injured? Were they dead? Thinking the words was too terrible, but she needed to know. "What did you do to my family?"

"Never you mind."

It was strange. Marianne had always shown kindness and mercy to living creatures. She never participated in gossip with friends, and normally defended the women who were ill-treated by Society. To have such a man find her strong-willed personality tempting and to think he would expect her to make a match with him was baffling.

She'd never allowed any of her suitors to kiss her. She made it known such an action was for her future husband alone. So, as she sat on this horse riding farther away from her family and all she held dear, she wondered how a woman who had protected her virtue so stringently had fallen into such a pathetic predicament. She vowed in that moment to fight Brockhurst with all her strength. And if this was the end of her life, so be it.

Four

LUCAS STOPPED FOR THE NIGHT WITH the hope of finding a bed without lice or bedbugs. It was the only coaching inn along the back road he'd taken in hopes of cutting hours off his trip and saving funds. Arranging for one night's lodging was simple. His room was terrible, even if it was for one night. The ceiling was stained from a leaky roof, making him thankful it wasn't raining. As a large rat scurried across the floor, Lucas shook his head in disappointment. This was the life he'd been reduced to due to his parents' lack of self-control. If he didn't take control of their finances soon, he wouldn't even be able to afford the run-down building in which he currently stood.

To take his mind off the miserable situation, Lucas found his way down to the main room in hopes the supper he'd paid for would be worth the extra coins. As he walked down the stairs, he held to the banister and found his gloves covered in dust.

He wasn't a snob, but it didn't take much to have pride in what a person owned, and he found it further disappointing to know the place was as poorly cared for worse than he'd originally thought. No matter how dire his circumstances were bound to become, he would always take care of the place he lived in. Even if he had to clean it himself. Of course, he wasn't certain how well he'd do at manual labor, but his goal was to take pride in his circumstances.

Lucas took a seat at a table in the corner and investigated the bowl before him, stew with a peculiar smell. He looked up to see the woman who'd brought the food stood waiting. He poked his spoon into the thick liquid and inwardly groaned before slowly lifting the spoon with the lumpy gelatinous cuisine into his mouth. It was worse than he'd expected. The extreme amount of salt and garlic tortured his senses and instantly cleared his sinuses. Taking great pains to keep an expression of disgust off his face, Lucas forced a smile and nodded his head in false appreciation.

"This is a fine meal. Thank you for your hospitality." Even though it wasn't the truth, Lucas decided there wasn't a need to injure the woman's feelings.

"We have more on the stove if you'd like a second helping." Her smile was hard to miss. He could only expect his fine clothing had left the coaching inn owner and his wife in anticipation of more money.

"Thank you, but one serving will be enough for my needs." As she turned to leave, Lucas looked back at the stew. It'd taken all his self-control to swallow and not spit the small amount he'd put in his mouth back into the bowl. Another inward breath, and the smell of overcooked cabbage told him his stomach would refuse the rest of the bowl. Lucas stood. "I am terribly exhausted. Thank you for the meal.

"But you didn't eat much. Does it need more salt?"

"No." The strangled words ripped from his throat at the same time a woman also cried out. He turned away from the cook and looked to the door to see Mr. Brockhurst pulling a woman through the door of the inn.

He knew Brockhurst by reputation only. The man had never crossed his path for an introduction, and Lucas preferred it that way. Rumors of Brockhurst's dealings with other members of the peerage had floated through Society; gambling debts was top of the list. Brockhurst didn't come from an overly wealthy family, and the consensus amongst the *ton* was he needed an heiress to resolve his financial concerns.

"Lud!" Lucas cursed under his breath. "What will they say about me?" It had crossed his mind more than once to seek out a woman with a substantial dowry. He was titled, which helped his prospects, but could he condemn a lady to a life of poverty while he worked to get Wymount's debts under control? He hadn't yet sunk so far. Eyeing the bowl of stew and the run-down furniture he stood next to made him reconsider that thought. He was much lower in his financial situation than he ever wanted anyone to discover.

"I need a room." Brockhurst pulled the woman close and whispered in her ear. Her naked leg slipped out through her ripped skirts causing Lucas to turn away. No woman should be shamed in such a callous manner.

Instead of calming, she pulled away from him and cried out while fighting to hold her skirt closed. "Please, help me. I beg of you. Do not let him keep me. My father will reward you handsomely."

Brockhurst put his hand over her mouth and pulled her close. Upon first sight, Lucas thought he might know the chit. But he hadn't a proper view of her face. Her auburn hair reminded him of a few women in Society, but it was a familiarity in her soft well-bred voice which caught his attention. Even if they were not acquainted, as a gentleman, he couldn't allow Brockhurst to treat a woman with such contempt.

Lucas stepped forward ignoring the chatter amongst the guests. "Brockhurst, what have you done to this woman?"

To Lucas's surprise, when Brockhurst turned toward him, hand over his captive's mouth, Lucas recognized her. His heart fell with concern. Lady Marianne, daughter of Duke Ashby and sister to his friends.

"Stay out of it, Branton."

Lucas knew he couldn't walk away. As a gentleman and a good person, he had to save her from the trouble she was in. He didn't understand what was happening, but the tears falling down her face and the terror in her eyes told him she was not a willing participant.

"I am afraid it is impossible. For I know Lady Marianne and her family intimately." He'd courted Charlotte, now Lady Haughton, the previous season. If she hadn't married Haughton, he was certain they would have made a fine match. But Charlotte's heart already belonged to the other man, and Lucas happily released her from their courtship.

"She is not your concern. We are married."

Lucas kept his eyes locked on Marianne's face as he spoke with Brockhurst. He could see denial in her eyes, and he wanted to let her know he understood. He also wanted Marianne to know she had nothing to fear, for he would not leave her with the vile man.

"I did not hear of an engagement. When was the marriage?"

"We were married this evening."

Lucas looked at their clothing. He could see Marianne was wearing a party dress that had seen better days. Had he taken her directly from the party? Did her family even know she was missing? "I assume you were at Almack's."

"Yes. I did not see you there."

Lucas shook his head. "I chose not to attend. But I am also fully aware that Duke Ashby would not allow his youngest daughter to marry you in such a manner. He would expect the banns to be read and a large gathering to celebrate her marriage. Allow me to escort Lady Marianne back to Watson Manor. You can speak with Duke Ashby in the morning about an arrangement."

"No. We are on our way to Gretna Green."

Lucas nodded. Lies were never easy to remember, especially in a stressful situation. "I thought you claimed to already be married."

"Innkeeper, is my chamber ready?"

Marianne whimpered and struggled to break free. Lucas wouldn't allow Brockhurst to take her to a bedchamber. The entire situation would inevitably bring ruin to the girl, but he wouldn't allow the rake to take her virtue. "It is best you give up now. Duke Ashby will destroy you if you choose to ruin his daughter."

"The duke does not genuinely care about his family. Her reputation will suffer for a short time, and all will be repaired by a marriage."

Lucas shook his head. "No, Brockhurst. Lady Marianne will accompany me back to London. I will ensure her safety."

Lucas had much he needed to do in Bedfordshire, specifically their home which was in Cardington, but this was more important. Marianne needed his assistance and although it would put a dent in his pocketbook, it was nothing to the security he could offer the poor girl in the moment.

Brockhurst shook his head. "I told you to go away, Branton. Do not make me use force."

Lucas looked to the innkeeper. "Please keep this man tied up until a constable can be brought."

"Yes, my lord."

This was one of those moments where his title did him justice. As an earl, Lucas instantly gained the upper hand over an untitled man. It might not be fair in all situations, but this time he didn't begrudge his position. Lucas watched as the innkeeper and two other men took Brockhurst, removing a weapon from under his clothing.

As soon as she was free of her captor, Marianne rushed into Lucas's arms. He'd never held a woman in such an intimate way, but knew she needed the reassuring care of someone safe. He could give her this comfort and so he ignored the rules of propriety as she clung to his body.

"I would like a private parlor. Lady Marianne will need food and water." Lucas reached into his purse and fetched the last of his coins. He didn't regret it because Marianne needed care. But he knew there would come a point when he would need to replace the money and he wouldn't be able to do so. The only regret he had while handing the last of his funds over was that his last meal had been heavy with salt and garlic.

Lucas waited outside the door until Marianne was ready for him to enter the private parlor. He would need to make plans for returning her to London. But for now, he wanted to ensure Marianne was not only physically safe, but emotionally calm.

When he was finally permitted to enter the parlor, Lucas found he was tongue-tied. Lady Marianne looked awful from the entire ordeal. He knew a physician should be called, but he hadn't the coins to pay for one. He would sell his horse, if needed, for she looked ready to collapse. She also needed a new dress. He hadn't the money to provide her with one, and so he removed his coat and motioned for her to cover her legs. Standing in his shirtsleeves was terribly uncomfortable, yet necessary.

"Lady Marianne, I will send for a physician. I apologize for not having already done so. Please sit and rest."

"Lord Branton, there is no need. I must offer my gratitude for the way you handled Mr. Brockhurst. If you had not been here, I do believe the nightmare would have continued." Tears poured down her cheeks and her lips quivered along with her hands. He'd never seen a high-born woman in such a state. "Thank you for assisting me."

Lucas held out a hand to calm her fears. He didn't know what to do with himself, for he'd never been in such a situation. "I assure you, my lady, there is no reason to fear Brockhurst any longer. The constable came and took him away. Ashby may do what he likes with the man."

"I dare not imagine what Ashby has in mind."

"Do you wish Brockhurst to go free?"

Marianne shook her head. "He is a vile man. I pray he is ousted from England. A ship to Australia is preferable."

Lucas found his lips twitching but held back the smile as this was not a moment for levity. He slowly made his way to the chair across from Marianne and sat. "You are safe with me. I will not harm you."

"I do not fear you, my lord. You saved my life."

A weight lifted from Lucas's chest as he saw the truth of her statement. She trusted him, which would make his goal of returning her to London much easier. Although she was tired, he needed to attend to logistics and assess their current situation. "Do you have a horse?"

"No. Brockhurst forced me to ride with him."

"Does anyone in your family know you were abducted?"

Marianne nodded as her shoulders shook and tears burst from her eyes. The words she'd meant to say were lost within an incoherent sob. Lucas had sisters, but he'd never comforted any of them. Handling an emotional woman was beyond his capabilities. But he did what seemed best. Lucas left his chair and knelt before the distraught woman.

"What can I do to relieve your suffering? Perhaps the innkeeper or his wife has a tonic to help you sleep."

"I need to go back to my family tonight. They could be injured or worse."

Although she hadn't mentioned her reputation, he knew somewhere in the back of her mind she had to be worried about the gossips of Society. Her reputation would suffer if she spent the night in a coaching inn with Lucas even if he stayed in a chamber down the hall. He didn't worry about his own situation, as soon as Society was aware of his father's financial troubles, it would outweigh this night.

"I am afraid it is too late to travel. I am certain your family is safe. I would beg you to settle in for the night and try to feel at peace. I will do all in my power to return you to Watson Manor on the morrow."

Lucas's words did nothing to lend comfort, for Marianne continued to cry. He held out a handkerchief, which was instantly soiled. Perplexed over her state and not knowing how to help, Lucas reached out and pulled her into an embrace. It was the only action he could think to do that might make a difference.

Unfortunately, as soon as he pulled Marianne into his arms the door to their private parlor burst open. Lucas turned to see The Duke of Ashby and his sons pushing through the chamber to Marianne's side. He knew in situations like this it was common for facts to become jumbled. As he pulled away and allowed Marianne to be swept into Lord Arundel's arms, he looked to Duke Ashby making certain there wasn't an accusation more aware of his state of undress than he had been before. However, there was no need to worry, even with his shirt-sleeves bare, Lucas stood before Duke Ashby as the man who'd saved Marianne.

"Lord Branton, we owe you a debt." Ashby held his hand out in a gesture of warmth that didn't reach his eyes.

Lucas took the proffered handshake and nodded. "I am thankful to have been of assistance."

"Gads, Branton," Edward called out as he patted Lucas on the back. "What are you doing in a place like this?"

He didn't think Edward needed an answer, or even wanted one. He gave a tortured smile to one of his oldest friends and then turned back to Marianne. Arundel was doing a finer job than Lucas had at settling his sister's nerves. Lucas hoped to never be in such a situation again.

"I am thankful I was here. Otherwise, there is no telling the condition she'd be in at this moment."

Ashby cleared his throat. "Arundel, you and your brothers will take Marianne to Earl Mannering's home. It is close by, and he will take us in for the night. Tell him Lord Branton and I will follow."

Marianne looked up with confusion. "Father, Lord Branton saved me."

Ashby turned and placed a very soft hand upon his daughter's arm. "There is no need to fear. I am aware of Branton's aid in this situation. I only wanted to thank him in private for his role in saving your reputation." Ashby turned to Edward. "See if the innkeeper's wife has a dress or outerwear to cover the rip in Marianne's dress."

Lucas' face heated as his coat was handed back to him. He stood waiting for Ashby's private conversation, dreading the moment he knew was coming.

Five

Lucas watched with envy as Ashby's sons obeyed. He knew Ashby was not an easy man to please, nor was he a loving father. But he was a father who had left the comforts of home to search for his youngest daughter.

It was hard for Lucas not to compare Ashby and Wymount. He knew if one of his sisters had been abducted, he would have to be the one to save her. Wymount wouldn't even leave his bed to pace his chamber in anticipation of the daughter's return. To Wymount, she would be lost and irretrievable. He would consider it one less person for living expenses.

"I think we should sit." Ashby interrupted Lucas's thoughts and brought him back to the musty smell of the rundown coaching inn.

"Yes, your grace." It was all Lucas could think to say. He moved back to the chair he'd occupied while trying to speak with Marianne. His cheek was still damp from the tears she'd cried while he held her in his arms.

"I want to get straight to the situation here. No member of the peerage stays at a place like this unless they have fallen on difficult times."

Ashby's callous way of questioning Lucas about his financial situation was surprisingly appreciated. It was easier to have the man suspect at the situation instead of having to say the words out loud.

"Where is Wymount?"

Lucas adjusted his position in the chair and looked away from the duke. "Lydney Hall."

"I haven't seen your father in Society for many years now. Why has he gone into seclusion?"

"I am not close to my father. He has not confided his reasons." Lucas wasn't ready to admit his father suffered from acute melancholy. He hoped one day the duke would pull out of his depressed state.

Ashby nodded. "I had heard of the apathetic nature of the duke and duchess."

There wasn't much Lucas could say, so he quirked an eyebrow at Ashby to show he was listening to the conversation. No one in Society had ever cared to question the lack of familial comfort within Wymount's family. What was behind Ashby's musings?

"I have an offer to make. One to save you and one to save my daughter."

Lucas knew what the man was doing. He'd arrived at the topic much swifter than Lucas expected. "Her reputation is safe, your grace. I have no intention of telling anyone of this night."

"But if my calculations are correct, you have need of my offer. Please, listen to what I have to say." Ashby stood and made his way to the window. "If I am correct, the cost of a private parlor and bed-chamber for Marianne has depleted the majority of coin within your purse. You quite possibly have nothing left for your trip and have little hope of refilling your purse without selling something of worth."

Lucas didn't know how the duke had pinpointed his dire situation so easily. It worried him that others in Society would do the same, and the results would bring a severe amount of shame to his family. He didn't respond as he couldn't bring himself to admit the extent of his situation, at least not yet.

"I have deduced this because a gentleman would have sent for a physician given Marianne's condition. Could you not even afford a country doctor?"

Lucas shook his head and pulled out his coin purse. His voice was strained as he had to admit to the poverty he now faced. "It is empty. I spent everything I had to bring a small amount of comfort to your daughter. If I am unable to restore my father's estate, I will be England's newest member in debtor's prison."

The smile on Ashby's face left Lucas in little doubt to his situation. He was stuck in the position of dealing with a man who was known for shrewd gambling. "Every last coin — gone? It is not surprising. I had heard the rumors."

Rumors? Lucas hoped Ashby was playing his hand instead of telling the truth. If word had spread about Wymount's finances, it wouldn't be long before debts were called in and his entire family was threatened with prison. He wished for a property to sell to correct the situation but feared they were all part of the entailment. His knowledge of the estates within his inheritance was limited due to Wymount's neglect in personally educating his heir.

"I hope you are more willing to listen to my offer, now we have brought forth the truth."

He was stuck in a corner with no way out. Lucas couldn't raise his voice above a whisper as he knew what Ashby would want. "Yes, your grace."

"My daughter needs a marriage for her reputation, and here you are, a ready-made earl in financial distress in need of a wealthy woman."

Lucas hated himself for asking the next question, but he needed to know what he would get from the match. "And what is the benefit for me?"

Ashby's eyes moved into a sharp focus. "A purse with enough coin to never run dry if you prove yourself more responsible than Wymount. I will even gift you Ashford Manor in Sussex. It is near Arundel Keep. You and Marianne can reside there until you inherit from Wymount. At that point, you may decide if you will keep Ashford Manor or sell it to pad your family coffers."

A warning bell sounded in Lucas's mind. Everything Ashby said was desirable and beyond any hope he'd had since discovering the depth of Wymount's debts, but was he making a deal with the devil? He needed to think about the entire situation before accepting anything Ashby had laid before him. "How long do I have to consider your generous offer?"

From the glint of satisfaction in the duke's eyes, Lucas knew he expected an acceptance. "I will give you until morning. We will post the banns and announcements will be sent in the evening post. You and Marianne will be wed by Michaelmas."

Lucas was thankful for the few hours he'd have to consider his choices. He stood, hoping to find Earl Mannering's home held more comforts than the inn. "I will have an answer to you by the morning meal."

Ashby held out his hand, which Lucas found unneeded. They were not shaking on a deal, as one had not yet been made. As he put forth his hand, Ashby opened his fist to show a handful of coins ready to pass to Lucas.

"I expect you have not had this much coin for some time. As my son, you will get used to a full purse."

Lucas understood his acceptance of the coins to be an acceptance of the marriage arrangement. It was far too tempting to pass, and he opened his palm to accept. The weight of financial worries lifted from his shoulders. He no longer had to wonder how he would pay for food, his servants, and general living expenses. Looking into the duke's eyes, Lucas nodded his agreement.

"Good. I hate waiting until morning for a decision. I will inform Marianne of her upcoming wedding when we reach Earl Mannering's estate. I will also send a rider to Wymount and inform him of our arrangement."

Lucas found the weight settling back upon his shoulders as Ashby led the way to Mannering's home. It was no longer due to finances, but it was the stress of bargaining with the man before him. Ashby had tempted him with money, and although Lucas hadn't betrayed anyone by accepting the coin, he'd shown Duke Ashby he was easily manipulated. A new stress entered his chest constricting his breath and it was worse than the financial distress he'd just relieved.

Six

MARIANNE HELD HERSELF TOGETHER DURING THE short trip to Lord Mannering's estate. She even kept her emotions subdued to offer pleasantries to Lady Mannering, but when she was in the bedchamber assigned to her, tucked away in bed with a borrowed night rail, Marianne allowed the pent-up tears to fall. She screamed into her pillow until her throat ached and when her bedchamber door opened and Phillip, Edward, and Charles came to her aid, Marianne allowed her brothers to offer comfort, but it did little good.

Her night had gone terribly wrong. She was supposed to be engaged to Mr. King. She should be in her bedchamber at Watson Manor comfortable within her own bedclothes. Instead, her head was buried in Phillip's waistcoat and Edward was pacing the room while Charles sat in helpless silence.

"Should I send for a doctor?" Edward asked.

"Yes. Charles, will you ask Lady Mannering if she has any sleeping tonics?" Phillip pulled her tighter into his embrace and lifted her head so he could speak to her. "Tell me what we can do."

Marianne responded with an ugly guttural sob. She tried to speak, but had nothing of worth to say, and so she stopped.

"Ask Lady Mannering to send up a cloth and a water basin as well." Phillip smoothed her hair back. "You will make yourself ill, if you continue to cry."

She didn't care. As a high-born lady of Society, Marianne knew it was her duty to be calm and collected in public. But in the privacy of a bedchamber, she could lose her mind and indulge self-pity as well as any low-born woman. It was her right as a human and a female.

When she could no longer cry, she realized Phillip still dutifully held her and Edward sat next to her wiping her face with a cold cloth while Charles rubbed her feet. She lay with her eyes closed as they whispered reassuring words she hadn't heard while in the depths of anguish but was now thankful they cared enough to let her know she was going to survive the entire ordeal.

"Is she awake?" Ashby's voice caused Marianne to open her eyes. She looked to the door as a movement took her attention away from her father. Lord Branton stood just outside the room behind Ashby.

"Yes, I am." Marianne pulled the quilt up in an effort of modesty.

"I have negotiated an engagement for you with Lord Branton. As he has family matters to attend to, we will post the banns and allow for a proper wedding ceremony."

Marianne sat up. All her hopes and dreams were quickly being torn away from her, but love was of the upmost importance. She needed to marry a man who loved her. This was not negotiable. "Lord Branton does not love me. I have spent these last years searching for a love match. I cannot give up now."

Ashby didn't care about love. He didn't understand the need for romance in a marriage. "A woman is to give her husband one gift upon their marriage, and you can no longer offer it to the man who will take you as his wife. Virtue is prized above all other qualities in a woman, and Lord Branton has chosen to accept you as you are, ruined and wholly undeserving of love. Be thankful I arranged a marriage with an earl who is heir to a dukedom. In your current state, you deserve a pig farmer."

"Asbhy, your words are too harsh. It was not Marianne's choice to be abducted. She is not ruined." Phillip pulled her closer protecting her from their father.

"In the morning you will take her to Arundel Keep. I will not see her again until her reputation is restored by marriage."

Lord Branton's movement into the room stopped Marianne from burying her head back into Phillip's already soaked waistcoat. "Your grace, please do not be angry with Lady Marianne. I was witness to the struggle with Mr. Brockhurst. She was not ruined, and her virtue should not be in question."

Ashby quirked an eyebrow. "Does Duke Wymount allow you to speak so boldly?"

"Wymount is too apathetic to speak as you do."

As Marianne watched her father and future husband stand in opposition of each other, she wondered if her father had matched her with a man as terrible as himself. She didn't want to marry a cold heartless man, but Ashby was correct when he told her she was no longer worthy of love. Brockhurst had taken everything from her, it didn't matter that she'd kept her virtue. He had stolen every chance of love from her.

Marianne left Earl Mannering's estate in a fine carriage with her father and brothers. She'd slept poorly, and her head ached, but she paid enough attention to know Lord Branton had stayed behind to finish his previous travel plans. Fighting the piercing pain behind her eyes, she couldn't help the questions filling her mind as she watched Branton and Ashby speaking while her brothers sat with her in the carriage.

Her voice was shaky and soft due to her night of crying. "Do you think Ashby forced Branton into the arrangement?"

Phillip took her hand and squeezed it for support. "No. I spoke with Branton this morning and he said the conversation was friendly and at no point was he under duress."

"He does not want to marry me. Why would he agree to do so?"

Edward answered this question for her. She was thankful it wasn't only Phillip working to convince her. "He is a gentleman and cannot help himself when he sees a young maiden in distress."

Marianne allowed a little laugh to escape. Edward was very sweet and funny at times. "Do you think he will regret his decision?"

Her brothers snorted in disgust, but Charles gave the answer. "Not if he is intelligent. You are the most admirable of all the available women amongst the *ton*. There is no need for concern."

Marianne hoped to tease her brother, but only a little. "Most admirable of available women? What about Lillian?"

This question stopped Charles from responding and made Phillip and Edward burst into laughter. It took Charles a moment to recover, but when he did, he shook his head in disgust. "You are fortunate I dare not retaliate, dear sister. After the night you had, it would be cruel."

"I am sorry for my comment. Will you forgive me?"

Charles nodded. "I already have."

Looking back at her father and Lord Branton, she had to know what was happening. "Will you help me down?"

"Why?" Phillip asked, not moving to do as she requested.

"I want to know what they are speaking about. Is Father threatening Lord Branton?"

"No. He would not do such a thing." Edward said the words, but he didn't look at her as he had before. She knew her brothers were also concerned over the conversation.

"Let me tell you about Ashford Manor." Phillip put his arm around her shoulders and pulled her tightly against him. "I do not think you have ever been there."

"No. I do not remember it." Marianne turned her head away from the conversation between her father and Branton and looked to Phillip. "Father said it is near Arundel Keep."

"Yes. Close enough for you and Branton to take supper at least once a week if not more."

Marianne smiled at the prospect of spending more time with her brother and sister-in-law. She knew Edward and Anne visited Arundel Keep regularly. It would be comforting to have family close by, now she was to be married. Although Branton wasn't a stranger, she didn't know much about him.

Marianne wanted to ask more questions about her future home in Sussex, but kept her mouth closed as Ashby climbed into the carriage. She shrunk into Phillip's side hoping to hide from her father's notice. Taking a seat next to Edward, Ashby knocked on the top of the carriage and within seconds it lurched forward to take them home.

"Arundel, I hope you learned the art of negotiation over the last hours." No one had to answer for Ashby to continue his speech. "I saw an opportunity and I took it. Branton set out last night intending to take care of estate business and ended the evening with an engagement. That boy had no idea what he was getting himself into. Wymount's neglectful rearing of his heir left him vulnerable."

Marianne's hopes plummeted even further. She knew love was no longer a part of her future, but did Ashby have to ruin everything by manipulating her future husband?

"I have known Branton since our days at Oxford. He was never easily manipulated." Phillip was agitated by Ashby's comments, so Marianne squeezed his hand now in support of her brother.

"You are probably right. But when he was at Oxford his family was not in financial ruin. He spent every last coin he had last night to rent the private parlor and a room for your sister."

"How do you know?" Marianne asked. She could feel the guilt spreading into her cheeks as they heated.

Ashby ignored her and continued to speak to Arundel. "There is no need to worry about his pocketbook now. I took care of the expenses. He has more than he needs to complete his trip to Wymount House. When he has finished his investigation, he will meet us at Arundel Keep. I think it is best your sister and Branton are married from there."

Marianne sat back against the carriage and buried her face in Phillip's arm tilting her head up so she could see out of the corner of her right eye. She didn't want her father to see the pain of his obvious poor treatment toward her.

"I am deeply concerned about this entire situation," Phillip said. "I do not agree with manipulating people into engagements."

Ashby laid his head against the back of the carriage, stretching his legs out, which made everyone physically uncomfortable. A perturbed sigh sounded through the carriage. "Branton knows what he is doing. He also knows the ruin his family is up against considering the path they are on. This was an opportunity for both Marianne's current situation and his financial troubles. He was not forced into the arrangement. He will benefit as much as we will from this connection."

"Or he will despise me for what you have done." Marianne should have held her tongue, but she couldn't leave her thoughts unspoken.

Ashby didn't open his eyes. Instead, he grunted and finally spoke to her. "You are the one who continued to accept offers to dance with

Brockhurst. I told you not to associate with the man, but you insisted on being kind. Do not blame me for this debacle. I have saved you from the scorn of Society by finding a match. You could show a bit more gratitude toward me."

Thoroughly chastened, Marianne took a moment to calm her nerves before responding. It was true she'd accepted one dance from Brockhurst at each party, but if she'd refused, it would have caused gossip. Either way, she was the one who'd lost in this situation. "I apologize for my outburst, your grace."

"You will be forgiven once you are bound in matrimony to Lord Branton."

Marianne looked to Phillip and then her other two brothers. None of them looked pleased with Ashby. It was a small consolation to have everyone on her side. It wouldn't change what Ashby had done by arranging a marriage. But now she understood why Lord Branton agreed to the marriage. He needed her dowry.

Seven

Lucas took a deep breath of relief as he exited the carriage. The ride to Arundel Keep with his mother and father had been torturous. The duke agreed to leave Lydney out of respect for Duke Ashby. Respect for his son's upcoming nuptials had no effect upon Wymount. Duchess Wymount insisted on new clothing for the trip and the wedding, which disappointed Lucas, but since he foolishly wanted his parents at the wedding, he'd acquiesced and allocated the funds for her use.

"Branton," Arundel said as he met the carriage. Arundel's limp, although not terrible, was the only way Branton could tell from a distance it was the earl. Phillip and Edward being identical twins caused a lot of confusion in the past.

"Arundel, thank you for the invitation."

"Do not thank me, yet. I trust your trip was without trouble?"

Lowering his voice, Lucas tried not to grimace. "Yes, other than having to spend the hours with the duke and duchess in an enclosed carriage." He knew Arundel understood. Lucas's father had never been abusive in the physical sense; emotional neglect did enough damage.

Arundel gave a low chuckle and nodded in understanding. Turning away, Lucas watched as Arundel did the proper duty of host and welcomed his other guests. "Duke and Duchess Wymount, welcome to Arundel Keep."

"Where is Ashby?" Wymount's question was abrupt and rude considering he hadn't accepted Arundel's greeting.

"He awaits us in the den. If you are not in need of rest, I can take you to him."

Lucas gave a tortured upturn of his lips that couldn't be construed as anything but embarrassment as his father grunted. "Let us discuss this business now. We will rest later."

Following his father's slow pace, Lucas prepared himself for the upcoming discussion. He and Ashby had left the negotiations of the marriage contract unsettled as there hadn't been time to call for solicitors. Lucas knew it would anger Wymount, but the dowry would be kept away from his parents. They would have to retrench and correct the issues with the estates before more frivolous spending could occur.

"Wymount!" Ashby said as though he were talking to an old friend. It wouldn't be surprising to know their fathers spent time together, but "friends" would be a stretch. Wymount had complained openly upon the invitation from Ashby and news of Lucas's upcoming marriage. He'd said words Lucas had only ever heard outside the dingiest of London's pubs.

"Ashby, what have you promised Branton to convince him to marry one of your brats?" Lucas wasn't prepared for his father to behave so boldly. "We are not destitute."

Pointing to chairs, Ashby moved to his own before responding. "I pulled your son, an earl, from a coaching inn filled with lice and rats. Do not pretend he chose to stay there for the scenery."

Wymount grunted and took a seat. "How much did my foolish son admit?"

"Nothing. He admirably listened and then accepted my offer. I suggest you do the same for if the stories I've heard at White's regarding your wife's extravagant expenditures are true, then you need more help than I am able to financially give."

"I have heard rumors of you as well, Ashby. You are not the soul of propriety as you intend to make me think."

"I admit to nothing for it is a pack of foolish rumors for the uneducated mind. Repeat what you wish, but there will be no proof."

Lucas hated the ruthless mind games high born men of Society played. He avoided places like White's due to the haughty men within the walls. His goal was to complete the marriage contract before the wedding was to take place.

"What are you offering my son? If the rumors I've heard of your youngest have any value, it better be a significant sum."

Choking on the drink Arundel handed him, Lucas coughed to clear the liquid until he could breathe again. "How could you say such a thing? The rumors hold no truth."

"My son is a bit of a prude. Calm down, Lucas." The laugh coming from his father told him he suspected the rumors were true but had no evidence or proof. This was a side of his father he hadn't seen in years. Lucas feared this discussion with Ashby could pull his father back into Society. The continued ruin such a prospect would bring upon their finances was unthinkable. Lucas wouldn't be able to control his father's spending, and the estates would suffer. "Brockhurst seems to have disappeared. No one has heard from him for over a fortnight."

Lucas rolled his eyes and looked away. The painful cringe on Arundel's face told him his friend understood the embarrassment Lucas currently experienced at his father's hand. Ashby's eyes focused on Wymount, his gaze emotionless.

"Father, I think it is best we finish the marriage contract before further offense is given." Arundel held out the parchment for Duke Ashby.

"Wymount, your son needs an advantageous match to keep you and your wife out of debtor's prison. I am offering him more than is expected." Ashby spoke with what he thought was calculation.

The lack of emotion threw Lucas off, but Wymount was ready with a response. "You wouldn't offer such a dowry if your daughter's reputation was whole." Without so much as a look in Lucas's direction his father started negotiations. "If Branton does not mind having a ruined woman, then you can make the offer.".

Wandering through the extensive gardens at Arundel Keep, Lucas mulled over the burden of his upcoming marriage and the continued dreadful state of his father's finances. He would one day inherit all of it, even the debt.

His life had changed drastically since discovering the financial problems within the duke's estate. Marriage to Marianne would fix all his current worries, but he was looking at it as a financial agreement. He knew she was distressed and hoped for love, but that was more than he could give. Anyone who knew his parents would understand his aversion to the word "love."

There was a fad going through the young in Society, worse than the fad Beau Brummell had brought upon men's fashions. The new way of thinking had young debutantes looking for relationships of love. Lucas hated the wretched term. No one in his life had ever shown him love, and he didn't understand how to give such feelings to another. The word was baffling and the source of all his troubles with women.

Although Marianne wanted love, it wasn't now possible. She needed a match, and if he hadn't agreed to it, then Ashby would have found another man to do the deed. One of Lucas's reasons for agreeing to Ashby's offer had been solely to protect Marianne. After seeing the emotional distress she was under, Lucas worried most men would willingly take the funds and land offered in the dowry and push Marianne to the side. He hadn't saved her from one rake to give her to another. With his temperament, he had the ability to do right by Marianne. He would treat her with respect and be generous.

He would be lying if he claimed the money held no sway in his final decision. To be financially secure was more than he'd hoped in such a short time. An hour before he'd saved Marianne from certain destruction, he'd thought it would be years before he could claim financial relief. But the security Ashby offered had tipped the scales in favor of the marriage, and now he was only days away from having a wife.

Even with the weight of his thoughts, he appreciated the haven Lord and Lady Arundel had created in Sussex. The vibrant fall colors in the trees and the luscious lawn sent a temporary yet calming balm through his mind. He could stay on this estate for the rest of his life, and never regret leaving London and all its so-called diversions behind. This was what he wanted for his future. A good and wise woman by his side, raising their children, and making a home for them in the country, but he didn't know what Marianne wanted.

He followed a path in the garden heading back to the house. He would have to request a meeting with Marianne. Rounding a bend in the hedge, Lucas stopped as he realized his query stood before him with her sisters. He'd found Marianne, Lady Haughton, Lady Arundel, and Lady Anne standing next to a garden fountain of cupid with an arrow aimed toward an unsuspecting mortal.

"Lucas!" Lady Haughton called out. He'd wanted to escape so he wouldn't interrupt their conversation but was wholly unsuccessful.

"Lady Haughton," he said, crossing the empty space between them. "I had hoped to speak with you more than small pleasantries this last season. Tell me you are well?"

"I am." She hit him on the arm. "I thought I told you to call me Lottie."

"It would be improper, now you are married."

She scoffed at his formal manners. "You are not only one of my dearest friends, but you are engaged to my sister. I refuse to go back to formalities."

"If you wish."

"I do." Charlotte motioned toward the other women. "You remember my sisters, Marianne, Anne, and Emma?"

He locked eyes with Marianne and found himself with an uncomfortable loss for words. She was changed since last they'd met. She lacked peace and startled with little sounds. Lost in his thoughts he missed the pleasantries of the other women and found himself in a silent promise. He would do all in his power to keep Marianne safe.

"Lucas, are you unwell?"

Turning back to Charlotte, Lucas shook his head. "I am perfectly fine. I apologize for my lack of attention. I have much on my mind."

"You have been distracted since arriving at Arundel Keep."

Lucas nodded. He didn't want to talk about his estate issues. He'd spent the last few nights pouring over ledgers and books focused on estate planning in hopes of rectifying problematic areas.

Lucas looked back to Marianne and although she was delicate in emotions, he found she stood with a silent strength. She was stronger than he'd expected. "Lady Marianne, may I beg a moment of your time?"

Marianne nodded her head and took his outstretched arm. "Yes, my lord."

He thought of the brief moments they'd spoken when he'd courted Charlotte. He'd known her as a lively witty woman who cared about others. The image of her curled up in bed, tortured and clinging to her brother out of fear and the struggle to get away from her abductor, left him disquieted. Lucas led her a short distance from the other women, so they could have a private conversation, but not too far for the sake of propriety. He wouldn't further compromise Marianne.

"I apologize for my lack of attentions over the past few days. I have much on my mind."

Marianne's lips turned up and her eyes brightened for only a second before the cheer left her pale face. "Lord Branton, I know what my father is asking of you, and I will not fault you for begging my refusal."

"I am an honorable man. I have agreed to the match, and I will do all in my power to see to your comforts."

Marianne shook her head. "I need a match but not if it was forced upon you by my father."

"I was not forced into this engagement. I accepted with full understanding of who Ashby is and what he expects of me." He thought about revealing his financial distress, but he didn't want her to think poorly of him.

Marianne blushed. He admired the pink as it started at the nape of her neck and spread upward. "My father claims my reputation needs a marriage. Without it, I am doomed to be the topic in every London parlor of the upper ten thousand."

Lucas looked into Marianne's haunted eyes. He could see the pain this situation had caused and didn't want to bring further injury, but he had to make certain she understood his position. He wasn't in love with her. This was a marriage based solely upon their mutual need for saving.

"I need you to understand, I am not in love with you, nor will I ever be in love with anyone."

"I am also not in love with you. But I hope we can move toward such an accord at a later date."

"I do not ever plan to be in love with anyone. I have no idea what it means and have no reason to believe after living eight and twenty years without ever having experienced the meaning of the word that it will suddenly fall upon me or knock me off my horse."

The disappointment in Marianne's features showed as she looked down and turned to the side. "Surly you could try to love me, once we are wed."

He couldn't agree because it would set an expectation he couldn't fulfill. When she realized he hadn't any understanding of the term love perhaps she would understand. He could promise her a good life. Much better than what he'd received from his parents. They'd fought regularly and pushed their children off on schools and servants. He wouldn't leave his future family to such a fate.

"I cannot promise love, but I can promise to treat you with respect and to provide for you and our future children. It is the best I can commit to at this time. Marianne, do not agree to a marriage with me if you have dreams of a man telling you he is in love with you. I am not the right man for such a sentiment."

She was conflicted. He could see the trouble building as her lips turned down and her shoulders slumped. Perhaps he'd been too forward in sharing his thoughts, but it was best she understood what a life with him would be.

"If we are married, in time we can find our way to London for part of the season. We will have a good life together. I will be generous. We could build a life of happiness."

Marianne's head came up, and he saw a glimmer of hope through the tears. "You would strive to be happy with me?"

"I would make every effort to bring joy into our lives."

"But not love?"

He wanted to back away and hide in the shrubs. Love was one of those words people said that meant absolutely nothing. Parents were supposed to love their children, but not all parents had such emotions. Husbands and wives were supposed to find love, yet he'd seen what marriage was like for his parents and aunts and uncles. He wanted none of it. Since he had to marry, he wanted the expectations clear from the beginning. Friendship was easier to come by than the enigma called love.

"I can commit to friendship."

He hoped it would be enough, especially given their circumstances. If they enjoyed each other's company, it would be much more than his parents had. He hadn't realized he was holding his breath in anticipation of her response until she nodded her head. It wasn't a verbal reply, but it was enough to let him know she understood his position.

"Lady Marianne, I am certain we can have a wonderful life together."

"Thank you, Lord Branton."

He needed to tell her of his financial concerns. Perhaps she would want a man free of Duchess Wymount's greed. "Duke and Duchess Wymount have long believed children are unwanted creatures. I cannot in good conscious allow my sisters to continue suffering at their hands. My father is apathetic towards us, and my mother is focused upon her own needs." He left off the bitter admission of their distaste for family. They'd never actually wanted children. It was only necessary to satisfy the title. "My sisters have been tucked away at schools for most of their lives. They do not have a proper home with my parents, and I prefer not to pay for their education within an institution. Are you willing to let them stay with us? It will be a permanent situation."

Part of his goal in rectifying their finances was to bring his sisters to Ashford Manor and provide a governess. It would save a great deal of money and he hoped it would allow him to know his siblings.

"I think it would be wonderful for your sisters to join us at our new estate."

Lucas looked down at the ground. This was the best he could hope for given his need for an advantageous match and her need for a husband. "You are too generous, Lady Marianne. I do not know my sisters. I have never spent time with them. It will be an adventure."

Marianne gave a genuine smile. The haunted look in her eyes changed and he enjoyed the sparkle of the sun within the blue. "How many sisters do you have?"

"I believe there is five, although there might only be four."

"You are not certain?" The shock and disbelief in her voice left him wondering what he'd done to disappoint her. His family wasn't anything like what she'd experienced growing up.

"No. As I said I do not know them. We were raised separately, and they are much younger than I."

"You will have a solid challenge ahead of you, my lord."

"What makes you say this?"

Marianne's smile brightened further. He'd never believed it possible with the pain he'd seen earlier. "You might possibly have five sisters and a new wife all under the same roof vying for your attention. I worry for your sanity. What makes you think there might only be four?"

Branton took her hand and started walking back to her sisters. They'd walked a distance, and it would be appropriate to take her back. "One of them fell ill a few years ago. She wasn't expected to live, and I never heard if she did."

"How terrible!"

Lucas nodded. It was horrible he'd never asked after his sister. He would be a better brother once they arrived. "Yes, I should have paid more attention."

"What are their names?"

A blush crept up his neck and into his cheeks. "I humbly and foolishly admit to not knowing all of them. I believe the eldest is Arabella and the one who was ill is Flora, but as for the others, I cannot remember their names. My parents never speak of them."

A glint of challenge entered Marianne's eyes. "We will have to change your relationship with your sisters, my lord."

He left Marianne with her sisters and left to meet with their fathers. In very few words, he agreed to the final marriage contract with the condition he'd previously planned. "I will control the investments made with Marianne's dowry." Finding the line in the contract where it gave the funds to the estate instead of him, he crossed the words out and wrote his version in.

Ashby puffed out his chest and produced a rolled-up piece of parchment pulling Lucas away from the contract. "This should help with the concerns of Wymount's estate."

Lucas took the parchment and read silently. When he realized Ashby had arranged for Wymount's affairs to fall under Lucas's care, he reread the wording before looking at the duke. "Why did you do this? I planned to make the arrangements."

"I have more influence than you, and it took less than an afternoon of cards at Whites to get the signatures needed."

"It was unnecessary for you to take the lead."

Ashby grunted. "Offer your gratitude and finish signing the marriage contract."

Lucas looked to his father and held out the legal document. "Are you aware of this?"

"Ashby informed me of the situation. I wish you had discussed the finances with me."

Holding his tongue, because it wouldn't do any good to argue with his father, he looked back at the marriage contract and searched for the line where he would sign.

As he signed his name with a flourish, Lucas looked at his father, a part of him regretting the words he needed to say. "Marianne and I will reside at Ashford Manor for the majority of the year. I will also take my sisters under my care. I will control the estates, pay off your debts, and you and mother will retrench. You will be given an allowance. I will not allow you to squander Marianne's dowry."

With the arrangements made, Lucas left to dress for supper.

Lucas stood nervously waiting for the carriage that would bring his sisters to Arundel Keep. It was terrible for him not to know his sisters and especially if Flora were still alive. Unable to bring himself to ask the duke, he decided it was best to wait for their arrival.

As the carriage rolled up the drive, Lucas found Marianne's hand slip into his. She squeezed his fingers in a show of support and then took a step away for propriety. This moment would be forever seared in his mind as he took on the responsibility of caring for his sisters. It wasn't more than other men his age had done. Many of his friends had lost their parents and were caring for land and siblings. His only problem was no one had ever taught him how to be a parent. Lucas was out of his depth.

Wymount approached the carriage as it came to a stop, the show of support to his daughters purely theatrical. Anyone looking on would think this was a commonplace action, much like escorting a woman into supper. But Lucas knew better. He knew his father and mother well enough to see they were uncomfortable.

His father helped each of the ladies out of the carriage and introduced them in turn. "Lady Arabella, Lady Mary, Lady Flora, Lady Alice, and Lady Victoria."

Lucas's heart lightened with seeing Flora, especially after not knowing if she were even alive. She looked frail and his worry mounted when a wheelchair was provided for her use. Looking to Marianne, he silently let her know with a glance he hoped conveyed his concern that this part of their life together would be a challenge.

When Marianne walked forward and embraced each of his sisters, he mused over thoughts of her being the only woman among the peerage who would have been so graceful. Taking courage from her example, he strode forward to meet his sisters. They would stay at Arundel Keep until he and Marianne were situated at Ashford Manor, but he would make every effort to know his sisters. He was all they had.

Before nightfall, Lucas and Marianne were married and, in a carriage, traveling to their new home, Ashford Manor. After he helped Marianne into the carriage, Ashby pulled him aside for one last word.

"Arundel told me you promised to let friends and family know you had feelings for Lady Branton while you were courting her sister?"

It was strange to see Ashby in a vulnerable moment, but Lucas knew it would not last long. Ashby wasn't one to linger over misfortune within his family. He'd go back to the gambling tables in London and forget his daughter had suffered at the hands of Brockhurst by the end of the week.

"Yes, your grace. I thought it best Lady Branton and I formulate a story we can share with others. Since the information about my father's finances can be quieted, I will make certain people who ask about my searching for a wife are informed it was merely gossip."

"You have thought of nearly everything."

"Is there something I have missed?"

Ashby looked him in the eyes. "Give Marianne time to become acquainted with you before exercising your rights as her husband."

This comment gave Lucas pause. Did Ashby care about Marianne? He had not considered going to her chambers as he didn't know her. She was the younger sister of a woman he'd courted. He'd never given her a thought while spending time with Charlotte.

"I give you my word."

With this agreement in place, Lucas walked back to the carriage and sat on the opposite side from his wife. Her lady's maid sitting next to her acted as a chaperon. Marianne only looked his way once, during the entire trip. Not knowing what to say or how to speak to his wife, he made himself as comfortable as possible and closed his eyes. It had been a long day.

Eight

MARIANNE FOCUSED ON THE LANDSCAPE OUTSIDE of the carriage as much as was possible, unable to force her eyes to gaze upon the man she would now call husband. If she did, a blush would escape her stoic features. She wanted to be everything he asked for; a friend. She knew Lord Branton to be a kind man. He'd saved her from what had been an impossible situation. She owed him her life. It didn't help to know her father decided to pay him for his assistance. Branton knew how to dance well and could converse intelligently in parlors and ballrooms. But she had reservations regarding this marriage. Now she was his wife, she realized there might have been more options they hadn't explored. If Ashby had allowed her a bit more time, she might have been able to find a man who could love her.

She debated on speaking to him about her concerns. He didn't want love in a marriage. He wanted friendship, companionship, and her dowry, which he hadn't admitted to her. Gaining courage, she peered across the carriage to see his eyes were closed. Drowning herself in sorrow, Marianne decided the only man who would marry a woman in her situation was one who needed money or, as her father said, a pig farmer. Branton stated love wasn't possible, and now she understood his meaning. He wouldn't be able to love a ruined woman. Tears threatened to spill but she wouldn't allow herself to cry in front of Branton. She would find a way to make her marriage happy so it would work for both of them.

Turning back to the window, Marianne focused on the setting sun. She could live with this decision and push all thoughts of what could have been away. She only hoped he would never regret his choice in her as a wife. She would make Lord Branton proud by giving him heirs. It was all men in his position wanted, when they didn't love their wives.

The serving staff stood at attention as they exited the carriage. She waited as Branton spoke to the butler and then took her husband's arm to enter the edifice. This would be her home for the foreseeable future. A place where she would raise children, build a family with her husband and his sisters, and host family and friends to their hearts content. They would be happy at Ashford Manor, until Branton inherited his father's estate and the title of duke. She told herself to be happy as she considered everything that would happen while living at Ashford Manor.

Now she saw the manor house, she understood her father's reasons for putting her there. It was a sad rundown home. Although large with extensive land, something was missing. Upon taking to the steps Marianne tested the first stones, hoping she was wrong. The Tudor constructed home was elegant to behold, but she was nervous as it looked unkempt; the stairs, door, and windows looked fragile. Nearing the top steps, Marianne let out a strangled cry as she confidently placed her weight upon the stone, and it wiggled loose. The crash of stone as it tumbled down the front steps echoed in her ears as Branton pulled her upright.

"Are you injured?"

Marianne quickly assessed her situation from her pounding heart to her dangling foot and shook her head. "Only startled."

"I will have the steward make the repair for your safety."

Marianne looked at her husband to see sincerity and surprisingly humor. She hadn't expected to see his brown eyes lit up in laughter. She also hadn't expected dimples. Branton had two perfectly placed dimples to highlight his broad smile. Voice shaking, Marianne gripped his arm for support. "I suppose it was a grand entrance into our new lives."

"A way to make a crash."

"You mean instead of splash?"

"Exactly."

Marianne laughed, finding the tension in her body releasing. Friendship didn't seem such a bad idea with Branton's handsome smile and pleasing manners. She placed her foot gently on the next step, testing it before allowing the full weight of her body. This action brought a deep husky laugh from Branton, and with that simple start to their marriage, they finished ascending the stairs and entered the home her father had given as part of her dowry.

Marianne groaned as she noticed the paper peeling from walls and dilapidated furniture. She looked to her husband hoping he didn't regret the marriage. It was far too early in their acquaintance for remorse. "This is a mess."

"I agree. But no matter. We survived the steps. There cannot be much worse within the walls."

Marianne wanted to argue but stopped herself before speaking. With such a statement it could only bring more misfortune. Considering the amount of work needed in the vestibule and foyer, Marianne surveyed the space; worn carpet, ancient wall hangings, and a musty smell would all need to be fixed. The home was ancient.

Marianne woke early in hopes of assessing Ashford Manor in greater detail. If they were to renovate, she would make a list of rooms and the particulars of each she'd like to see updated. Since it was early, and Branton had not yet emerged from his chambers, she walked the halls looking into each of the main rooms surveying everything from the carpet to the ceiling. There wasn't anything she expected to leave untouched.

Assigning bedchambers to each of Branton's sisters, she again noticed the amount of work that would need to be completed. She couldn't have those beautiful girls displaced from everything they knew moving into a rundown manor. But, she thought, they might enjoy picking out the fabrics and colors for themselves. It could make the transition easier and offer a friendship early in their acquaintance.

When she entered the music room, she found a profound sense of sadness in the dilapidated space. The piano was small, and the seating worn. The draperies were a putrid green, tattered, and in need of replacement. As she considered options for restoring life to the room, a feeling of excitement for the first time since leaving Almack's the fateful night of her abduction entered her soul. Marianne set to work writing out details of items she would need to make the music room beautiful.

"Mrs. Harwood?" Marianne said as she entered the housekeeper's rooms, "I have a list of items I will need from the shops in town." She handed the parchment over, pride swelling in her heart at her performance of Lady Branton.

"We did what we could with what the duke gave us." The bristly tone of her words gave Marianne pause. Was it an insult to the housekeeper to have the new occupants updating the house so soon after arriving?

Marianne nearly apologized but stopped herself. Why should this woman be offended? Ashford Manor was a wreck. Taking on the tone of the mistress of the manor, Marianne stood tall and looked the housekeeper in the eyes. "My father is no longer lord and master of Ashford Manor. Lord Branton and I inherited it upon our marriage. Now, will you kindly send someone to town for the items I have requested?"

The housekeeper's head reared back in offense. "Yes, my lady. Is this everything? Or do you have more?"

Marianne second guessed the tone she'd used. Mrs. Harwood's stunned reaction made her think there hadn't been a need for such a strong response. Taking on the role of mistress to such a large estate wasn't as easy as she expected. Over time, she would find her place and hopefully come to understand each of the servants.

"I only meant to say I wanted to put my touch on the home. Thank you for your help with gathering the materials." She'd watched her mother interact with servants and there had always been a level of respect between the housekeeper and the duchess. Marianne wanted to gain the respect of the housekeeper due to her kindness and ability to lead. She didn't want the staff to fear her. "Have you seen Lord Branton this morning?"

"He left an hour ago to survey the land with the steward. Should I send for him?"

Marianne quickly shook her head. A war waged inside her mind. She wanted to see her husband and speak with him, but she also feared conversation and saying the wrong words. If she slipped and hoped for more than friendship, would he be unhappy?

"We set out the morning meal. If you would like, I could prepare a tray."

"Thank you. I will take it in my chambers." Turning with as much grace and poise she'd witnessed in her mother, Marianne found her way back to her bedchamber.

"I hope you do not mind, but I plan to start updates inside the house." This was the only topic she could think of to speak with her husband. She still found a shyness around him, as they were not well acquainted.

Branton looked up from his meal. He sat at the other end of the table, far enough away to have privacy. She'd never liked silent meals. Even when her father would demand silence, she and Charlotte would whisper.

"I think that is a wonderful idea."

"I am starting with the music room."

"Do you not think it prudent to start with the rooms my sisters will stay in? Or perhaps the rooms we are currently using?"

"I wanted your sisters to help with the design in their own chambers. And I can start with other rooms if you would prefer." Marianne thought about going back to her food, and finishing in silence, but decided to speak again. The music room was important to her. She'd spent her entire life surrounded by soul-filled tunes. Ashford Manor would be dreary without the sounds of her favorite melodies. "I seem to remember you enjoy music. I thought the music room would be a wise choice for beginning."

"I do enjoy singing. I do not play an instrument though." He gave her a warm smile. "You play the piano."

Blushing at his words, she nodded, "Not as well as my brother and sister. But I do enjoy the exercise."

Branton cleared his throat. "I did not mean my question to be a criticism. Please do the renovations in the order you would like. What other changes do you have planned for the manor?"

This was not the most uncomfortable conversation they'd had since the wedding, but it certainly wasn't smooth and enjoyable. Marianne tried to think of other rooms she'd noticed. Although Ashby and her family hadn't spent any time at Ashford Manor, it seemed strange to allow the manor to fall into deep disrepair.

"The carpets are ancient and worn. I truly believe they were placed here during Henry VIII's reign."

The response was exactly what she wanted. Branton laughed. That same deep husky sound she'd so enjoyed the day before filled the room. It was genuine and heartfelt. "I tend to agree with your assessment. I think a renovation is long overdue."

"I am surprised to see some of the rooms in such disrepair."

"I agree. I plan to ask Ashby about it when we next see him. Until then, I think it is a task that will keep you long occupied."

Marianne frowned with worry. Her father would not appreciate the confrontation. "It might be easier to avoid bringing up the house. Ashby is not one to care about such things."

Branton set his fork and knife on the table. "Would it not be prudent to discuss his lack of respect for you and me? He claims to care about you, but a home in this condition shows the opposite."

Marianne looked around to see the curtains were torn, the fireplace mantle was chipped, and the chandelier was missing multiple pieces so most of the candles couldn't be lit. Branton was correct, but Ashby would not see reason. "I worry my father will tell you it is your fault for not checking on the estate before signing the marriage contract."

"There was not time. He knows I am focused on my father's estates to increase profitability. Ashby must be brought to see reason."

Marianne didn't want to argue with her husband. They'd been at the manor only one day, but she knew this was not a battle to pick with Ashby. "Perhaps, in the future you will understand my father.

For now, please trust my word when I tell you a confrontation with Ashby will not end well."

"It does not need to be a confrontation. I found Ashby reasonable during our previous encounters."

"He needed you to marry me. His goal was to make you think he cares. He does not."

Branton shook his head. "No. I have seen neglect in my own parents. Ashby has a different way of showing his concerns for his family, but I believe he wants the best for each of his children."

"Only in the eyes of Society." Marianne didn't want to speak negatively of her father, but Branton didn't understand.

"Then he will want to know about Ashford Manor. For if word reaches London that he put a rundown home into his youngest daughter's dowry, it will be cause for scandal."

Marianne chose to ignore this final statement because it didn't matter what she said to guide him on speaking with Ashby, he wasn't listening. Instead, she went back to the renovation. "Would you like to assist with restoring some of the rooms?" Marianne hoped he'd accept. It could be a project to work on together. Something they could do to help them become acquainted and grow toward friendship. She also hoped he would see her value as a wife and trust her advice.

Branton gave her a smile as he quietly gazed upon her. He looked to need a moment to decide if he should accept her offer. Or she thought he could be annoyed with her change of conversation. "I am terrible at decorating. If I had it my way, everything would be orange."

"Orange? What a horrible color to use in any room of the house. Perhaps I do not need your assistance after all."

She blushed as he smiled in her direction. The unexpected humor sent a nervous flutter through her heart. Avoiding his gaze, she looked down to the food. It was a delicious meal. They had a wonderful cook, whose talents hadn't been used for far too many years. She picked at what was left on her plate until Branton was finished and was pleasantly surprised to find he didn't want to stay in the dining room for port.

"Tell me more of your planned renovations." Branton took her hand and placed it in the crook of his arm.

Unnerved by the closeness, Marianne rambled her response. And changed the order of updates. She would take his advice and start on a room other than the music room. "I think it is best to start on the rooms most used and then move to those that will be used upon the arrival of guests. I will start with the parlor, drawing room, dining room, music room, and the bedchambers."

She blushed and looked away. Speaking of bedchambers wasn't appropriate in such an intimate setting. Although married, they were decidedly keeping separate rooms.

"I like the list you have set out."

Hoping to bring a semblance of balance to her nerves, Marianne looked back to him as they sat in chairs near the fire. "I will remember to decorate the earl's rooms in orange."

"You would not subject me to such torture after claiming it is an undignified color. Have pity upon my dull soul."

"If you wish it."

"I do."

Marianne knew she was blushing, but this time she didn't turn away. She wanted Branton to see her admiration. As silence grew between them, Marianne pondered over the words he'd spoken at dinner. His view of her family was from one on the outside. He saw her father as a person who tried hard to be a parent but constantly muddled the situation. It might be true, but she'd never considered Ashby to be a father figure or role model for others to emulate. She hoped Branton would see Ashby for what his was without causing the duke anger.

Nine

Lucas excused his valet then crawled into bed. It made him happy to know Marianne found a project to occupy her time and mind and he was even happier to hear she had thought of him and his sisters. The land needed attending, which he could do in the early hours of the day, leaving time to oversee workers for improvements on the outside of the manor. He would also see to hiring the workers so his wife could focus on decorating.

With this plan, he settled against the soft pillows and closed his eyes. Even with all of the work planned for the near future, he found hope in the budding relationship he and Marianne were building. He was nearly asleep when a soft knock sounded on the door joining his and Marianne's chambers.

Heart racing, he called out. "Come in."

The door squeaked with the lack of use. "Lord Branton, I admit I am not tired. Would it be an imposition to speak with you a little longer?"

Initially his mind drifted to propriety, but they were married. No one would question their nighttime assignation. Crossing to the plush light blue armchairs near the fire, Lucas motioned to one and waited for Marianne to sit.

Lucas took a seat. As he settled against the back of the chair, he gave Marianne his full attention. Her hair was down from its usual coiffeur. Her maid had tied papers in the auburn strands. This was a new experience for him. He'd never given thought to how women cared for their hair and achieved the beauty he enjoyed. He'd always taken for granted the curls, but now found there must be a bit of torture involved as he wasn't certain how the papers would be easily removed. Also, there was a question of comfort while sleeping, perhaps this process of achieving curls was why his mother always claimed a headache.

"Is there anything in particular you would like to discuss?"

As he said the word, "discuss," the back of the chair moved. Lucas repositioned himself and sat further back hoping for comfort. He expected to find the plush cushion of the chair, but instead, he howled as his entire body fell backwards and he tumbled to the ground, landing on the back of the chair as it lay on the floor.

"Lord Branton!" Marianne cried out.

"Lud!" Lucas said, before bursting into laughter. It was easier to find humor in the situation instead of giving into the pain.

This was quite possibly the most ridiculous situation he could imagine for himself. Marianne stood over him her hand outstretched to help him off the floor. He thought to take it, but she was laughing so hard her hand shook while hanging limply in front of him. He found her light airy laugh to be contagious.

"I never imagined a chair could be so faulty." Branton rolled to his side as he extricated himself from broken pieces strewn upon the floor.

The light in Marianne's eyes made him genuinely happy. He imagined what it must have looked like to have him fall backwards his feet and hands flying in the air, which only served to bring more lighthearted amusement to their evening.

"Your feet went over your head so quickly. I truly did not know what was happening. For a moment I thought it a prank."

"A terrible prank. I promise never to purposefully make my feet do such a horrendous act again— if I can manage it. Do you think I'll have a dignified injury to show off when company visits?"

"What, pray tell, is a dignified injury?"

"Arundel limps. I find it adds personality to the earl."

"My brother limps because his leg did not properly heal. Who else has an injury to brag about at supper parties?"

Lucas made a show of talking to himself which pulled more laughter from his wife. "Mr. Nordfelt is missing an arm."

"An injury from war. Please do not tell me it is a source of entertainment during parties. The poor man."

"No. No. We have never laughed about it or even held discussions. But it is well known he is a brave man, and his injury is proof."

"Then you hope to have a visible injury from falling off a chair? I do not think anyone will see it as brave."

"You are right. No one will think I slayed a dragon by falling off a chair."

"Dragons? You are too imaginative, my lord." Marianne suddenly stopped laughing and turned frighteningly solemn. "Can you believe two dangerous happenings at Ashford Manor within the first days of our arrival? Perhaps it is a terrible omen of our future. Do you think we are cursed?"

"Why ever would you think such a thing?"

Marianne turned away. Tears rolled down her cheeks. Allowing her the time to gather her wits, he waited. The quiet between them stretched out as he considered the possible reasons she would come to such a conclusion.

"Our marriage is a product of ruin. Perhaps Ashby is right, and I deserve nothing more than a marriage of convenience devoid of love and filled with tragedy. Shakespeare had it right when he wrote plays like Romeo and Juliet. Love or the appearance of the state of love does not come without trials and tribulations. If everyone had a perfect life, then there would be no opposition, and no one would realize their lives were built on sturdier ground than others around them."

He allowed Marianne to speak until she ran out of words. Each statement gave him more to be concerned over, for how was he to calm her fears? Lucas considered what he could say, and what he should say. There was so much ambiguity in their current situation. They weren't a love match. There wasn't anything he could do to change it, especially because he didn't know how to love.

"I know you and your siblings give Shakespeare center stage in the libraries of Duke Ashby's estates, but I must admit I find him tiresome."

"Tiresome?" Marianne shook her head in disgust. "How could you say such a thing?"

"I stand by my assessment." Lucas hoped she could see he was teasing her. "I also do not think we are given harrowing experiences, such as what you went through to bring judgment or punishment upon us. It is Society's rules and misguidance causing the fear within your heart. Our marriage is one of necessity, but only because we bowed down to the station we were born into."

"Society can be cruel."

Lucas pulled her close. He wanted to look directly into her blue eyes to let her know this next statement was the complete truth. "I can see our future when I look into your beautiful eyes. One of these days the greatest romance will be written to rival that of Shakespeare and even the current romance authors. They will look back on our beginning and think exactly what you do now."

"They will see a lack of hope?"

"No, my dear Lady Branton. They will see two people struggling to stay positive in the cruelest of situations. A lady who dreamed of finding a love match ruined by the jealousy of a rake and a lost earl who did not know love was important until he married the lady. But together, they built a life worth sharing."

"Do you truly believe everything you have just said?"

"I hope for it to be true." Romance and love were not the same thing. He could make her feel special by giving her flowers and little gifts. Those were the foundation of romance from what he'd seen in Society.

He lifted Marianne's hand to his lips and kissed her knuckles. A desire to pull her fully into his embrace spread through his arms, causing them to shake with nervousness. He wanted a full marriage, but knew it wasn't the time. Marianne could confuse his desire for her to be love and he wouldn't cause her injury. It was best they said goodnight. Walking her to the door separating their chambers, Lucas watched as she crossed the room and made her way into bed. Before closing the door, he quirked an eyebrow and tried to say with all seriousness the quip hanging on the tip of his tongue.

"I trust you will take precautions when testing the chairs by your fire. I would not want you to find your feet above your head. It is an unnerving situation."

"I will be careful."

As he took hold of the doorknob to pull the door shut, it broke away. Lucas held it up for Marianne to see with a mischievous smile upon his face.

"I must be extraordinarily strong."

With Marianne's laughter following him to his own bed, Lucas found his mind cleared of all worries regarding the estates and his father's finances. The broken furniture, doorknob, and front steps should concern him, yet it was his wife occupying his mind and blocking sleep. He would make an effort to figure out what she wanted when it came to the word love. He might never be able to feel such a short and strange word, but he would try. Whatever it was she thought was love, he wanted to give it to her.

She deserved his every effort.

Ten

MARIANNE HELD UP THREE SWATCHES OF fabric, each a variant shade of yellow, for Branton to choose from. She knew which one would be perfect for the parlor but wanted to give him a chance to share in the design. His indecision put a smile on her face as she watched him lick his lips in concentration.

"I am terrible at such things. Do you not remember I suggested orange?" He took each swatch in hand and held it against the wall. The pink clashed terribly with all three. "We are removing the pink in full?"

Marianne held out the lightest shade. "Yes. It would look comical otherwise."

"I agree." Branton examined the colors again, bringing a smile to Marianne's face. She was very happy he allowed her to show him color swatches. Even if it only brought laughter. "Comical. Yes."

Seeing his indecision had hit a wall, Marianne pointed to the lightest of the fabrics. "I think this one will be perfect. The morning sun will shine through those windows and brighten the entire space, once we remove those ghastly window dressings. We need not use candles in the early hours if I am right."

Branton nodded, kissed her forehead, and took the swatch in hand. "I agree. You have an eye for design my dear."

Marianne found heat rising in her neck. She had to look away from her husband so she could stop the blush from fully forming. She didn't know what had caused him to place a kiss on her head, but she'd enjoyed it. Holding up a sheer lace material, she tried to force the flutter of excitement out of her stomach so she could continue speaking. "I like this for the window dressings."

"It will look lovely."

Over the previous days they'd shared lighthearted laughter. The only serious conversations had been focused on Ashby and love. She'd avoided all discussion of Ashby since that terrible supper. But it was hard to repress the thoughts surrounding love. She was convinced her changed circumstances made her fully undeserving of a love match. She was only thankful Lord Branton had taken her as a wife. Marianne enjoyed the way he'd taken to calling her my dear. Her growing admiration for the man she'd married would be one sided, and she hoped it would be enough to last her lifetime.

"I want to rid the room of the threadbare carpet. Also, this shade of pink is atrocious. It will take little effort to reupholster the cushions on the sofa and the chairs." She looked over to Branton with a mischievous smile. "Do you want to test each before I start the redecorating to make certain they are sturdy?"

The boisterous laugh from her husband brightened the putrid pink surroundings. Marianne watched as he made a spectacle of himself sitting on each piece of furniture to test the endurance. They had enough funds set aside to purchase new furniture when needed, but she hoped to be wise in her spending. She wanted to show Branton she would be meticulous to the point of frugal. She knew his mother had overspent, but she didn't know any details and Branton hadn't been forthcoming with any information on his finances.

Marianne tried not to giggle as Branton made a scene of checking under each chair. He lay on the ground in his shirtsleeves wiggling each chair leg, tapping on the underside of the cushions, and pulling on the backs. When he finished with one, he crawled on the floor to the next. For an earl, he looked utterly ridiculous but somehow her thoughts of him increased in esteem.

When finished, Branton hopped to his feet and brushed the dust from his clothing. "The carpet needs a thorough brushing."

Hand over her mouth to hide the increasing smile on her face, Marianne shook her head in delight. He would need more than a hand brushing to rid himself of the dirt. Seeing the state of his clothing, she wondered what the maids had done while the house was unoccupied. Had they accomplished any work?

Marianne walked to her husband and helped brush off the dust. "Perhaps we should hire new staff. I do not think there will be any love lost amongst the current group. They do not seem happy to have us here."

"I would like to give them the opportunity to acclimate to our presence. It must be difficult having new owners present when the previous never visited."

Branton was right. There was a lot of wisdom in his statement. She decided a short discussion with the housekeeper was in order. "Do you think it would be appropriate to ask the housekeeper to focus on dusting the entire house from floor to ceiling?"

"You are very wise, my dear."

Marianne walked to the bell cord and lightly pulled the string. Instead of finding resistance, the material fell on her head with a collection of dust. Coughing to clear her throat of the grime now covering her mouth and tongue, Marianne forced back tears. This was not how the occupation of Ashford Manor should have started. She and Branton were supposed to be enjoying each other's company by becoming better acquainted. Instead, they found humor in every problem within the house and used it to avoid actual conversations on important topics.

Branton must have noticed her quivering bottom lip as he rushed to her side. "I must thank this cord for falling so abruptly upon your head."

"Why?" She held the sob down and grimaced at the dirt in her mouth.

"I now know what you will look like when we are old with grey hair. You will be lovelier than I could have imagined. But now, I will ask your maid to draw a bath."

"Thank you."

She stood still in her spot while he rushed from the room. She needed a moment to collect her wits. Although all the broken items were easily fixed, the stress of their situation was not lost upon Marianne.

As she soaked in the warmth of her bath, Marianne wondered how long Branton would be able to continue with seeing the humor. At some point, one of them could be seriously injured. She wanted to curse Ashby for giving her a dump to live in. She decided to persuade Branton no longer toward silence with Ashby, for if he didn't confront the duke, she would.

Eleven

Lucas wanted Marianne to see the beauty of Ashford Manor, especially after her mouth had been filled with dust. He could well imagine the tears shed during her time in the bath as he remembered the quivering of her lower lip. He'd been proud of her as she'd bravely held in all hysterics. It hadn't been necessary, although he wouldn't have known what to do if she had cried. Memories of trying to comfort her in the coaching inn came back, and he wished he'd asked Arundel for advice.

Overwhelmed by both his wife and the repairs needed on Ashford Manor, Lucas found his responsibilities to be much different than expected. He'd been raised as an heir, but his father hadn't given him practical knowledge to run an estate. Neither had the classes he'd taken on the subject at university or the book learning offered by his tutors. He found the process to be much more physically draining than the theory.

"Will you walk in the garden with me?" He knew she loved flowers and hoped it would calm her nerves.

Marianne agreed, so he led her out into the sun. He'd seen the gardens from afar. Overall, they looked well cared for and safe, if anything at Ashford Manor could be considered safe.

"Do you have a favorite flower?" He'd never had difficulty speaking with ladies, but now as a married man he wondered what topics were appropriate. Discovering her likes and dislikes was the easiest approach.

"I love forget-me-nots."

There was that word again, love. It was used so interchangeably between people and inanimate objects it invalidated any meaning. Instead of sharing his thoughts, Lucas silently made his arguments against the term.

Marianne continued. "I also love wildflowers. Do you think there is a possibility the gardens would have such an unruly flower within?"

With exaggerated intrigue, Lucas leaned toward Marianne and whispered. "Anything is possible at Ashford Manor."

They shared a laugh, which made her face light up. All tears were gone. He'd found a small amount of success and inwardly congratulated himself. With little effort, he led her into the nearest garden and then realized it might have been a terrible suggestion. From afar, the gardens looked lovely. Up close, the lack of care was obvious with plants strangled by weeds. Lucas turned to Marianne to see her eyes wide with shock and he wasn't certain if it was pain for the destruction of nature or sadness at the lack of flowers.

"Do not be distressed. Everything dies in the fall. We can find a gardener to restore the grounds and by spring we will have beautiful gardens."

"I hoped to bring flowers into the house to brighten the rooms. With the neglect of the gardens, I will have to wait until next year."

Having lived in his private rooms in London for many years he'd envied his married friends who talked about the little things that made a home comfortable. Suddenly he yearned to have flowers in the parlor and embroidered knickknacks on tables. He could see their future filled with warmth like they were wrapped in a comfortable blanket sitting before the fire. He might be thinking too far in the future, but he could see Ashford Manor filled with children, all of them with Marianne's auburn hair and blue eyes.

"I hoped to bring a little joy into our day. The parlor was a bit disappointing, but this was even more." To apologize for this blunder, Lucas decided he would find a hothouse to present Marianne with flowers.

"Oh look!" Marianne's exclamation took his attention away from the weeds. Lucas focused in the direction of her finger to see a lone white daisy rising above the mess before them. Marianne moved away, lifting her skirts as she rushed across the path. "It is a Michaelmas Daisy."

Deciding it was best to follow, Lucas rushed forward to assist his wife. He didn't pay attention to the cobblestone path, or the mud on the ground. He simply wanted to see Marianne's joy when she approached the only living plant within the garden. Watching her every move, Lucas veered off the path and found his foot sliding forward. Before he could catch himself and correct his balance, Lucas fell hitting his head against the stones.

Pulling himself off the ground, he was thankful Marianne was so intent on the daisy she hadn't noticed his fall. Brushing the mud from his clothing, Lucas rushed forward with a little more care for where he was placing his feet. His head and body hurt, but he didn't want Marianne to worry. So, he brushed off the pain and focused on his wife.

Ashford Manor would be the death of him, Lucas was certain of it. His head and body ached from the fall in the garden. Part of him wanted to ride to Arundel Keep and negotiate a new home, but he'd taken the estate unseen and that was his fault. He should have insisted on viewing the property before signing the marriage contract.

Slowly walking to a hot bath in the hope that the pace might keep the aches from resurfacing, Lucas prayed the heat from the water would sooth his injured body. Lowering into the water was simple. He adjusted to comfort and allowed his valet to pour a bucket of warmed water over his head.

"This is heavenly." The words were out of his mouth right before a loud crack sounded in the room. "What was that?" Water sloshed and some spilt over the edge of the tub as Lucas sat up. He'd heard too many strange noises at Ashford Manor to be content with ignoring anything suspicious. Lucas looked to his valet for an answer.

"I do not know, my lord."

"Grab my robe. I prefer not to be in this state if something is about to break." The noise was too familiar for any other assumption. Loud cracks meant chairs breaking, stairs eroding, and— Lucas stood placing his weight to one side of the tub and realized after it was too late that the crack had been the ancient bathtub his valet had brought in for his use.

With another loud crack the tub tipped to the side. Lucas quickly exited the water as it tipped and emptied onto the floor.

"That was a near accident, my lord."

Lucas nodded. He wouldn't have been hurt badly, but with the injury he sustained earlier in the garden it wouldn't have been a treat. He wanted to laugh and ignore all of the issues with Ashford Manor, but he was in pain. He would laugh in the morning as he told Marianne about this latest trouble.

As he thought of Marianne, he knew she'd used the tub at least twice since arriving at Ashford Manor. Was he so much heavier than she? While dressing for bed he pondered over the mishaps and disrepair of Ashford Manor. He would speak with Ashby when given the opportunity.

Twelve

Lucas wasn't certain how to handle the carriage ride to Arundel Keep. They'd been invited for supper, as it was a neighboring estate. If he sat on the opposite side of the carriage from his wife, would it continue the emotional distance in their marriage? If he was presumptuous and sat next to her, would she be uncomfortable?

The easiest way to solve this concern would be to speak with Marianne. If he asked for her preference, it would show he was being considerate. But did she want him to have to ask? During his time courting Lottie, he'd never had such reservations. But Lottie hadn't been abducted by a rake and she'd willingly accepted his courtship.

After assisting Marianne into the carriage, he stood trying to make the decision of where to sit. Her maid wasn't accompanying them, as it wasn't necessary. When he'd stayed out of the carriage long enough to draw the attention of his wife and the footmen, Lucas decided he would take the chance and sit next to her. If she were visibly uncomfortable, he could easily switch sides, and all would be well.

A glance at the crest of his title on the side of the carriage brought thoughts of his father and mother. They also had a marriage of convenience. One that was never strong nor wanted. It was common amongst the *ton* for people to be miserable in marriage and his parents had obviously been unhappy his entire life. She'd used him for his wealth and had drained the family coffers.

When he finally took his place, Marianne seemed to understand his hesitation. Being the strong woman, he'd seen over the past week, he shouldn't have been surprised when she laid a hand on his. Taking hold, Lucas turned to look into her eyes. They'd been honest with their feelings one time. Could he share all his worries with her now? Should he share it before attending a dinner with her family?

As the carriage jerked and rolled forward, Lucas chose to confide in his wife. It was the only way to move forward. Secrets were destructive in a marriage. "I worry your family will see we are still uncomfortable in our situation."

Marianne nodded. "It has been on my mind as well."

"I suggest we handle this in the manner of which Society would expect."

"But this is my family. We are not going to Vauxhall."

Lucas nodded in understanding. But he continued with his thought. "I prefer others do not see into our marriage. It would be distressing to think anyone is speaking of our discomfort."

"I understand. What would you like?"

"We could play a role."

Marianne laughed. "I think you are referring to Shakespeare. He did say 'All the world's a stage and everyone is an actor.'"

Lucas squeezed her hand to show his appreciation. "I never connected the two thoughts."

"So, we are to act well our part?"

"Yes. As an earl and countess, we are to have a certain amount of confidence. Therefore, we should not hesitate to join hands, sit next to each other, or speak positively of our situation."

"I can do this."

Lucas wanted to make certain he wasn't forcing her into deceiving her family. "Are you happy?"

"As much as any woman can be in my circumstances."

This response brought a pause to his thoughts. "I know if you were given the opportunity to make a match in London, it would not have been me. But is a marriage to me so distasteful that you cannot find happiness?"

The question should've waited until they were home, in their bedchambers. It was terrible timing to ask such a thing while on the way to a dinner party. Sniffling, Marianne took a moment to respond. He pulled out a handkerchief, berating himself for making her cry.

"I am very thankful to you for saving my reputation. I only meant it wasn't a choice for either of us and we are both in a situation of discomfort."

"I should not have asked such an unfeeling question."

Marianne shook her head. "It is best we share our honest feelings. I cannot live a life of pleasantries hiding behind lies. Tonight, and every night until we are more comfortable in our situation, I will play the part of countess you ask, but I do expect to find ourselves in a better situation in the future."

"What do you want from our union?" Lucas needed to know her expectations. They'd tiptoed around the word love. He was honoring Duke Ashby's request to give her time to heal from the ordeal with Brockhurst, but he needed to know what she wanted.

"I want love. I know I am wholly underserving of such a sentiment and yet I hold out hope that one day you and I can come to love each other far more than the greatest lovers of all time. When you spoke of a romance being written about our lives, were you in earnest?"

Lucas knew he never should have prattled on about books and romance. He should have left Shakespeare to the dust in the library. But it was still his hope. "Yes. I was."

"Then that is what I want, Lord Branton. I want you to love me. For I know I am bound to fall in love with you, especially if you continue to break doorknobs and fall backwards out of chairs."

He appreciated the humor in her voice and found it was timed perfectly for their arrival at Arundel Keep. When the door to the carriage opened, they were smiling at each other. The genuine picture this painted for Lord and Lady Arundel and Duke and Duchess Ashby as they met the carriage was far more pleasant than a forced smile for their titles.

Dinner was lovely. The company even more so. Lucas followed Arundel into the drawing room after port and conversation to find Marianne on the sofa with Arabella and Mary nearby. Flora, Alice, and Victoria were much too young to be eating in the dining room. Seeing an open spot, he moved toward Marianne and sat comfortably next to her. The warmth from her body left him tongue tied as he realized, he'd missed her.

"I would like to play a game of whist. Anyone interested?" Edward asked. He held the cards up to indicate he was serious. "Anne plans to stay in her chair dozing, so I will need a partner. Phillip?"

Marianne put a hand on Lucas's arm to stop him from rising. She turned and whispered. "They have some sort of twin intuition. No one has ever beat them at whist."

"Would it not be fun to try?"

Marianne shook her head. "No. It is disappointing, to say the least."

"Come now," Arundel said rising to join his brother. Lucas knew at some point he would need to refer to Arundel as Phillip. They'd been friends most their lives, but it did seem odd to call him by such an informal name. Same with Haughton. Although, he wasn't the only one who continued to use Haughton's title. Arundel and Edward seemed to struggle with switching to Haughton's Christian name as well.

Haughton stood to join the twins. "My wife refuses to play. Branton or Charles, which of you will join me?"

Charles shook his head. "Not a chance. I prefer to play a game I can possibly win. We all know those two are undefeated."

As Charles smiled at Haughton, Lucas turned to see if Arabella or Mary wanted to play but found the girls fluttering their eyelids at Lord Charles. Lucas didn't know his sisters, at all, but he was certain they were far too young for flirting. He would need to take the girls under his care and help them understand propriety.

Marianne nudged his shoulder. "They are young. Allow them to dream."

"And what of Lord Charles?"

"He is courting Lady Lillian Calder."

"You mean to tell me Haughton's sister is courting your brother, and Haughton has not lost his mind?"

"He finds it amusing."

"I have only recently met my sisters. I will wait to find such instances amusing."

"Branton, will you play opposite me?" Haughton asked.

Lucas squeezed Marianne's hand. He was adept at whist. She didn't know him well enough to claim her brothers would win. "I would like to, with Lady Branton's approval."

Marianne raised her eyebrows and smirked in his direction. "Do not cry to me when you lose. I warned you against their twin connection."

Lucas kissed her hand and crossed to the table. Sitting opposite Haughton, he motioned toward Arundel and Edward. "I think we can take them down."

Haughton's smile was forced. "I agree."

It was a short statement, lacking humor. He didn't understand Haughton's reserve but hoped to lighten the mood. As the game started, Lucas was surprised to find the diversion had nothing to do with cards.

"We wanted to speak with you, Branton. Without Marianne getting curious." Arundel said, placing his first card on the table.

Lucas looked to him and played a card as well. "Would not after dinner port have been a better time for such a conversation?"

"If Ashby hadn't been in the room, then yes."

Haughton and Edward seemed content to let Arundel lead the conversation. Lucas took his cues from them and continued to play while listening to Arundel.

"Marianne seems happy. Her smile upon your arrival was genuine, but I could see she'd been crying. What happened?"

Lucas groaned inwardly. This was a matter between he and his wife. "Nothing you need take concern over."

"And yet," Edward said with a smile that would make anyone looking on think they were enjoying the card game. "Marianne is not one to cry over insignificant matters. She is strong and intelligent."

"I have seen those attributes in my wife since we were wed. The tears were momentary and are not of any concern."

"Yet, we are very concerned." Haughton threw a card on the table while staring at Lucas.

Lucas looked down at the card and shook his head in disgust. "Are you trying to let them win? You played the lowest number possible."

"I have never been good at whist. I despise this game."

Lucas shook his head. He'd hoped to dissuade the conversation from going back to Marianne's tears, but it was in vain. Arundel, Edward, and Haughton glared at him. They were waiting for him to spill the contents of his marriage on the table.

"Lady Branton believes she is undeserving of love and affection due to the situation with Brockhurst. To say it has been a hurdle in our marriage is an understatement. We have not found a way through the barrier."

"Undeserving of love?" Arundel said throwing another winning hand on the table.

Lucas could see the twins, although concerned for their sister, planned to win the game. They would not only win at whist, but they would pull every private conversation between he and Marianne out of his mouth. It was good he was a gentleman with only land and a family to care for. He couldn't keep a secret if his life depended on it. It was best he stick to herding sheep at Ashford Manor with his wagging tongue.

"I am working to convince her this way of thinking is not accurate. But speaking with her on such subjects brings the hopes of what she once wanted, a marriage of love, to the surface. It is painful."

"Why do you not love her?" Edward asked.

For a moment Lucas thought Edward was jesting, but he wasn't. His mouth set in a straight line told Lucas his answer would need to be perfect. "We were married for convenience. Give us time to sort through the emotions of such a situation. Love, whatever it means, does not come with the marriage license."

Lucas wanted to add information regarding the renovation to the list of trails in their marriage but divulging everything at one time was too much. He needed to focus on one aspect of the challenge before them.

Edward looked to Arundel. "I fell in love with Anne the moment I met her. Was it not that way for you and Emma?"

Arundel shook his head his lips turned up in a smile. "We cannot all be as foolhardy as you, Edward." Turning to Lucas, Arundel continued. "I understand what you are saying. I agree with you, love has to grow. Please tell me you are working toward such an outcome?"

Lucas could with all confidence say he was looking for friendship, partnership, and accord. Love was firmly out of his reach. Elaborating would divulge the lackluster history of his childhood, so he didn't. But a firm answer in the positive was enough to convince Arundel of Lucas's intentions.

Thirteen

It was nice spending time with her family. The release of angst while Branton was playing cards with her brothers nearly took Marianne back to weeks before when she was in London. Her life had completely changed since then. She sat back and looked at the decorations around her. Emma had placed her touch on Arundel Keep, which made it a home. This was what she wanted for Ashford Manor.

At one time the drawing room at the Keep had been a lime green. It now sparkled in varying shades of blue. Marianne hoped when she was finished with Ashford Manor it would be a place to be admired.

"Arundel." Ashby held out a piece of paper. A letter he'd probably kept for that exact moment. "An announcement from one of my colleagues. His son has an heir. I am the last of my acquaintances to be without another generation of heirs for the title I currently hold."

Marianne had hoped her father would keep such conversations private until Branton had more time to know her family. She looked to Arabella and Mary and found they were too busy whispering and sneaking glances at Charles to be affected by Ashby's outburst.

"Your grace, when my wife and I have any news to share on such a situation, we will inform you."

Ashby threw the letter into the fire. "You do not care about my legacy or the legacy of the four Dukes of Ashby from the time the title was entrusted to us. If you did, you would make haste with bringing a male child into this world."

"I do care about my ancestry."

"Then it is me you do not care about? You prefer to have me embarrassed and unable to show my face in front of men less wealthy and powerful than I?"

"I care very much about your reputation."

"Do you not understand your duty?"

Phillip sighed. This was a conversation Marianne had witnessed many times between her father and brother. "I do care about your reputation. It is all I think about when I am looking over the affairs of the title."

"What do you mean by that?"

Phillip looked up from the card game and turned toward their father. "I know I am a disappointment to you. Please feel free to say as much and then we can continue this night without further discussion of all the ways I have failed the estate."

Marianne stopped breathing. She looked at Branton to see his eyes wide with shock. What would he think of her family? Would he regret his decision to marry her? Even if he did, there was nothing he could do about it, unless he chose to distance them from her family. She wouldn't be able to survive without her brothers, sisters, and mother. She could live without Ashby.

"I want you and your wife to understand the importance of bringing an heir into the family."

"We understand."

"Then why does she refuse to give you an heir?" Ashby turned toward Emma and glared. "My son chose you for love. If he had married Lady Olivia, I would have a grandchild by now. Instead, he married a barren woman."

Phillip stood facing their father. Marianne grabbed hold of Charlotte's hand out of worry. Ashby's anger could only be pushed so far. Phillip standing up to the duke was always frightening, as Ashby didn't care for disobedience.

"Emma does not refuse to give me an heir. It is I who refuse to do so."

"You are making excuses for Lady Arundel. I can see how much you want a child as you spend time with Branton's sisters. You have taken them into your home and made them your wards while your wife keeps her distance. I heard you discussing the situation with Edward. You want to keep the girls here for a while yet. She is the one who does not want a child. Do not try to convince me otherwise."

Phillip shook his head. "You are wrong. I have my reasons for not wanting children. Branton's sisters are welcome to stay for the rest of their lives, but I will not bring a child into my home as an heir."

"Why? What is your reason for this?"

Phillip stood taller than she'd ever seen her brother. Ashby was the only man he'd feared, and she could now see such emotions were behind him. He was ready to say what he needed, and he didn't care who heard. "I will not turn into you. For you are all I have as an example of the term 'father,' and I will not subject a child to such cruelty. I trust Edward and Anne to provide an heir, and I will have nothing to do with raising the future of this title and estate."

Marianne knew this would not turn out well. She looked to her mother hoping there was a way to stop the argument and any resulting abuse. The pained expression on her mother's face told Marianne she wasn't the only one worried.

Looking back to her father, Marianne wanted to cover her eyes and peak through her fingers. It was easier than looking directly at the man. His face was deep purple and the anger flashing in his eyes made them look red, she knew it was probably an effect from the flames in the fire grate, but the illusion was frightening. Preparing for the duke's anger to explode, Marianne was surprised to see her father retake his seat and wipe at his eyes. There were several responses she expected to see from the duke, but tears were not one of them. Ashby's color returned to normal as he nodded with an air of defeat. He motioned to the walls and turned back to his son.

"Everything you have is due to four generations of our family staying strong. If I had allowed my brother to provide me with an heir, you would not have this home. Do you understand?"

Phillip didn't allow their father's moment of defeat to bother him. Marianne could see a glint of defiance in her brother's eyes. He knew weakness would only encourage Ashby's cruelty. "It came at a cost. I am unwilling to pass abuse and neglect to another generation of this family."

"What if Edward's wife only provides daughters? What will you do then?"

"Charles has yet to marry. If he doesn't take a wife, then Haughton and Charlotte will provide me with an heir."

"Haughton has the marquisate to worry about."

"They may have other children. Charlotte looks to carry at least two or more at this time. More than one son cannot inherit and therefore, the younger can inherit your titles. If it does not happen with them, Branton and Marianne can provide. Someone within this family will provide an heir for the title and estate or it can pass to a cousin."

Ashby slammed his fist upon the side table. Marianne jumped as she hadn't expected Ashby's morose mood to switch so suddenly. From the corner of her eye, she saw a visible reaction throughout the room as everyone startled.

"We are part of a rare breed in the history of England. Never has a younger son inherited the title of Duke Ashby. Now you tell me you plan to pass everything I have built to a nephew of no rank. Edward's children will not have titles. Charles's children will be even further from titles than Edward's. They will be fortunate to be considered amongst the gentry. I will not stand for the insult upon our family name."

Marianne expected an angry retort from her brother. Instead, Phillip shook his head in disgust. "You believe we should live and behave in certain ways because Society dictates the rules. What about what each of us wants?"

"The possibilities for your futures are endless due to money and my position in Society. Without both, you would be living in the gutter."

"Perhaps the gutter is what some of us want."

She knew Phillip wasn't serious. None of her siblings would choose to live in such dire straits. But it was obvious they didn't need all the money within the family coffers. Ashby had enough to give to charities, if he chose to do so, yet he didn't.

"What of your sisters? Would you have them despised in London parlors throughout the *ton*? We did everything we could to save Lady Branton from such a fate, and now you disregard all my efforts in securing a match. With an earl who will inherit the title of duke no less. Most women in her situation end up in a cottage or feeding pigs on a farm. Instead, there are few people in London who know of her ruin, and I have done all I can to stop the gossip."

The words were cruel, but they solidified everything Marianne had thought about herself from the moment she'd woken to find Brockhurst had succeeded in an abduction. She was unworthy of the man her father had convinced and paid to take her off his hands. Unable to hold in her emotions, Marianne put her head in her hands. She didn't want Ashby to see the tears brought on by his callous words.

As her shoulders moved with her sobs, Charlotte's hand reached up and pulled Marianne close. Although Marianne was devastated by her father's cruel reminder of her circumstances, the compassion from her sister helped calm the pain. Marianne thought it would be best to hide in the corner of the sofa but stopped in her movement when Branton spoke.

"Thank you for the fine supper and hospitality, Lady Arundel. I think it is best we leave." Branton took her arm, helping her to her wobbly legs. When she staggered with despair, Branton put his arm around her waist and escorted her from the room.

Ashby would never forgive her for the scandal she'd brought on the family. He would remind her at every opportunity. She would take the rundown country manor and a man who might one day love her over lavish parties and a position in the Society her father cherished. London held nothing for her, now she was considered ruined.

Fourteen

MARIANNE PAUSED BEFORE PULLING HERSELF OUT of bed. She wanted to lay in the warmth of the covers while pondering over the previous evening. She and Branton had returned to Ashford Manor earlier than expected, instead of spending time with her husband in the parlor, she had gone to her room to try and sleep. She hadn't slept well. Ashby's words echoed through her head the entire night reminding her that more than a bit of gossip had reached London. What could her father do to stop the chatter? The matrons of Society would relish any gossip on a scandal of such magnitude.

It would be easier to stay in bed. She could hide away from life and her station. If she wasted away, Branton could find a new wife. One worthy of his impeccable reputation. Marianne nuzzled under the blankets to a comfortable position. She would take breakfast and all future meals in her bed.

With a knock on the door, Marianne called out for the person to enter. She looked to the door leading out to the hallway expecting a maid. When the door remained closed, she pushed up to her elbows and saw the knob-less door between her chamber and Branton's moved toward her.

"Are you ill?"

"No."

"When you didn't come down to break your fast, I worried you were under the weather."

"I am fine. Thank you for the kind inquiry."

Branton walked closer to stand beside her bed. "Do you plan to leave your chambers today? I hoped to ride over to Arundel Keep this morning. I need to discuss the situation of my sisters and Ashford Manor."

Marianne took a moment to decide how to tell him he was married to a shut in. For she would not go out into Society any longer, even to Arundel Keep would be an issue. His sisters would suffer from her reputation, and therefore he shouldn't bring them to their home. There was no way to sugar coat her words, and so she shook her head.

"I plan to stay abed, forever."

"Forever?" The hesitation in Branton's voice put a smile on her face.

"Yes."

"What about the plans for renovation?"

"I will no longer entertain guests, so there is no reason to spend the funds. If you would like, you may go back to your ancestral home and care for your sisters there. I will use this as my prison away from Society."

"You are referring to Duke Ashby's cruel remarks last night. I do not blame you for being hurt, but you cannot allow it to destroy the life we plan to build."

"What do you suggest I do? Go about Society ignoring the blatant remarks upon my reputation?"

Branton nodded his head in understanding. "Perhaps you are right. Seclusion is our only option."

"I knew you would see it my way." Marianne sat up in bed as Branton moved to a chair and removed his boots. "What are you doing?" Branton removed his outer coat to reveal his shirtsleeves. Marianne blushed.

"Move over, my dear. If you plan to hideaway in this chamber, then I have no other option than to stay with you. You are my wife and I promised to stay by your side. I do believe we said until death we part. I will have my valet ride to Arundel Keep and ask Lord and Lady Arundel to take my sisters under their protection permanently."

"You cannot be serious."

"I am in earnest. Scoot!" He motioned his hands to emphasize the last word.

With a large smile on her face, Marianne moved over in the bed. Branton climbed under the covers and lay next to her on the same pillow. Laughing, Marianne ignored the crack of wood and a slight shift in the bed frame. She expected it was due to Branton's movements as he adjusted for comfort. With an even louder crack, Marianne turned her head to see Branton had done the same. They stared into each other's eyes for only a second, but it was enough to see his concern matched her own.

"I think we should get off the bed." Branton said. He sat up and took her hand as the frame gave way sending them tumbling to the ground smashed amidst the feather tick, bedsheets, pillows, and anything else within the bed.

Shocked, neither of them made a noise. Marianne wanted to laugh, cry, and call out for help. But what did one do when she was tangled in bedsheets caught in a hole that once was a bed?

Branton put his hands under his head. "This is comfortable."

Marianne burst into laughter and fought to sit up, but it was impossible. They were stuck. "Help me out of this mess, my lord."

Branton laughed. "Not until you agree to a few concessions."

"I suppose it depends on what these concessions are."

"If you do not agree, we will stay in this state until a maid finds us."

Marianne slugged her husband in the shoulder. "What will our servants spread about the neighborhood?"

"Then you will agree to everything I ask?"

"If I didn't know better, I'd think you cut the bed frame to cause this mess."

Branton put a hand on his chest in mock horror. "I would never, my lady."

"Then name your price for helping me out of this ridiculous situation."

Branton held up a finger. "First, you will forget about seclusion, and we will rejoin Society together."

"Do you promise to be by my side at each snide remark sent in my direction?"

"Yes."

"You will not complain about having to attend garden parties and soirées?

"I will delight in your company."

Marianne bit her bottom lip as she considered his earnest expression. He was committed to her. "Then I agree." It brought her a small amount of joy to know he cared enough to make her position outside of their home bearable as one of his stipulations for getting out of the crumpled heap they were in.

"Second." Branton held up two fingers to indicate his list of requirements. "You will call me Lucas from this day forward when in our home and amongst your family. When formalities are needed, I dare not risk our reputations at this time. But I do prefer my Christian name to my title."

Marianne could heartily agree to this stipulation. She loved his Christian name. A secret hope rested within her chest as she looked into his glee filled eyes. She hoped he would ask to use her Christian name. She could offer it, but the current conversation built thin layers of hope that Lucas was falling in love with her. "I agree."

He held up a third finger. "Third, you will allow me to call you Marianne."

The smile spreading across her face had to tell him she was happy. She hoped he noticed the melancholy from the previous night had left her soul. "I had hoped you would ask."

"Fourth, we will never tell anyone about the bed breaking in such an unromantic fashion. Nor will we divulge the shameful situation in which we currently find ourselves."

Marianne blushed profusely. "I promise never to offer the information. But if I am asked directly, I will not tell a falsehood."

Lucas quirked an eyebrow. "What constitutes a direct question?"

Marianne laughed. "Oh, I believe the question would need to be along the lines of, did your husband jump into bed to convince you not to be a recluse? A direct question of that sort would be unbearable not to answer."

Lucas held his hand out. "We should shake on these four concessions."

His easy manner made her cheeks sore as she was always smiling. She didn't want a handshake. She wanted to show him how he'd made her feel. Instead of taking is hand, Marianne plucked up her courage and kissed him on the cheek. "Thank you, Lucas, for helping me to see the silliness of my ways."

Lucas cleared his throat and took a moment to respond. She hoped his hesitation was due to the intimate kiss she'd given him, and she hoped he had enjoyed the moment. Even with that hope, she allowed doubt to creep into her mind. Was he disgusted with her forward behavior?

"It was my pleasure." His voice was husky, which put a blush on Marianne's face. She had to distract him.

"How do you suggest we get out of this mess?"

"I will try to stand and then help you to your feet."

Lucas pulled himself into a sitting position, which forced Marianne to lie flat. When he tried to stand, Lucas fell backward, narrowly missing her head. She tried to help him by offering her hand, but when they both dissolved into further laughter, she was certain they would be found by a maid. The excuses they could offer would sound as ridiculous as the predicament.

Holding onto a piece of wood poking through the feather mattress, Lucas was able to gain balance. He held his hand out for Marianne. Forgetting her feet were tangled in the bedsheets, Marianne managed to pull him back down and for a moment they lay side by side giggling like school children.

"I think this house is cursed." Marianne said, hoping to elicit more laughter from her husband.

"I must admit it is a possibility."

Again, they laughed, but Marianne had to wonder if there was truly something wrong with the house. She'd slept on that bed for over a week without any problems. But the weight of two people sent them crashing to the floorboards. There was certainly something wrong with Ashford Manor.

Fifteen

His back hurt. He was certain falling through the bed had injured his already tender and bruised muscles. As he walked into Arundel Keep to discuss his concerns and his sisters, he was unable to stand properly. His right shoulder sagged, and his hips ached. But even with all his injuries, Lucas was content. Marianne filled his thoughts, and he couldn't wait to arrive back at Ashford Manor to spend more time with her.

"Has the burden of caring for your sisters finally settled upon your shoulders?" Ashby asked with a malicious smirk spread across his pious face. Ashby had made a name for himself by being an insufferable duke. But, since his standing in Society was far superior to most, his behavior went unchallenged.

"I admit it makes me nervous." To say he was nervous was an understatement. A new wife and sisters he'd met very few times was frightening. Marianne had proved to be a kind and levelheaded woman, but they had only been married a short time. He worried the stress of having his sisters at the house would break the bond he had started building with his wife.

"Arundel tells me they are delightful creatures." Ashby gave a forced smile.

Lucas stood waiting for the moment Ashby would turn into the duke Marianne had described. He'd seen a spark of Ashby's anger the previous night, and he wondered when the duke would next explode.

"I am certain he speaks the truth." It was the only response Lucas could think to say while standing lopsided in front of the man. His head hurt from the strain in his back and from falling in the garden. "Do you know what is keeping Arundel and my sisters?"

"I told Arundel I wanted a word with you. My daughter seemed distressed last night. I do not like seeing my daughters in such a state."

The man had nerves far beyond that of a king. It took everything within Lucas for him not to lash out at Ashby. Marianne had been happy, until Ashby expounded on his disapproval of her ruined state. "Perhaps if you stopped disapproving of your children and their actions, you might find their happiness not to be a burden."

Ashby's lips thinned and his eyes focused upon Lucas. If his own father hadn't been so neglectful, Lucas might have been intimidated by the duke. But he found Ashby to be an annoying bully.

"Marianne's happiness is all consuming. I have done much to squelch the rumors regarding her abduction."

Lucas tried to hide the headache drawing nearer to the surface. He didn't want Ashby to think his taunts had any sort of affect. "Perhaps if you left all comments of the situation with Brockhurst in the past, Marianne would not be reminded of the situation. It was distressing enough, without having it brought up during a family dinner."

"My children owe me for their happiness. I have done all I can to secure their futures."

Lucas had no doubt about their financial needs, but emotional needs were entirely separate. He'd known Arundel and Edward far too many years to know the duke wanted happiness for his children. "I will do all I can to bring joy to my wife barring help from you." As he said the words, he knew deep within his soul he meant to keep the promise. Her emotional needs were a top priority, even to resolving his financial concerns. It was strange but invigorating to be so affected by a woman.

"I saved your family from debtor's prison. Do not forget the benevolent dowry I bestowed upon you. I have also allowed your sisters to stay at Arundel Keep."

Lucas knew his sisters' stay at the Keep had nothing to do with Ashby. But he couldn't deny the length Ashby had gone to with the dowry, and the debt had been great. His father's situation worried Lucas. It was constantly in the back of his mind.

"I thank you for your intervention with Wymount and his debts. I will thank Lord Arundel for the care of my sisters. As for Ashford Manor, there is much we need discuss."

"You have the funds to restore the estate. Do not bring such concerns to me."

Lucas took a step away and ran a hand through his hair. Ashby was fully aware of the ruinous state of the manor. He'd hoped there had been a mistake. There was a part of Lucas that wanted to accuse the duke, but he remembered Marianne's admonition to keep silent on the issues of their estate for it would only spark Ashby's temper. He would need to apologize for arguing about Ashby. She was correct in her assessment of the man. "I will say no more of our current housing situation."

"I think it is best. If you would like my advice on Wymount's estates, I am willing to look over the books."

"I appreciate your offer." He never intended to ask for Ashby's help. He might consult with Arundel, but his father-in-law was not to be trusted. Hoping to move away from the topic of finances, Lucas turned to the only other question he could think to ask. "I do have one other question for you. Brockhurst, what was done with him?"

Ashby's lips spread into a pleased expression that some might confuse for a smile. Lucas knew better. The glint in Ashby's eyes showed his sinister pleasure over the punishment inflicted upon Brockhurst. "He is none of your concern. No one will concern themselves with that man again."

Instead of pressing the matter, Lucas nervously nodded his head. Ashby wasn't someone he wanted to cross. Turning to the door, Lucas pushed his worries away as Arundel carried Flora into the parlor on his back with the other girls following and Lady Arundel pushing the empty wheelchair. Flora had hold of the earl's untied and backward cravat treating him like a horse.

"Do not stop, Phillip." Flora's use of Arundel's Christian name put a smile on Lucas's face. It was wonderful to see his sisters smiling and laughing.

"Where is your sense of pride?" Ashby's booming censure put an end to all laughter. "You are an earl. Can you not behave with propriety?"

Lucas walked forward and took Flora from Arundel's back. He carried her to the wheelchair, noticing a sadness reenter her face.

"Ashby, I thought you were to speak with Branton in my den."

"I chose to stay in here and I think it was best seeing the way you have behaved. One would think you were a child."

Lucas didn't care for angry words. His parents spent more time neglecting him and his sisters than speaking to them. Such confrontations were unnerving. "Arundel, thank you for the kindness you have shown to my sisters."

"It is easy to do. They are a delight to have in our home." Arundel looked around then back to Lucas. "Marianne is not here?"

"No. She has much to do at the manor." Lucas took a deep breath. He needed to speak about his sisters and make plans to remove them to Ashford Manor, but he hoped to keep them at the Keep until the manor was safe. It seemed the wrong conversation to have after the tension with Ashby.

"Emma and I think it would be nice to keep the girls here. They seem happy and we enjoy their company. It will give you and Marianne more time together."

Lucas turned to Emma. It was hard to forget the words spoken the previous night when Ashby claimed Emma wanted nothing to do with the girls. He could see she was reserved around them, but the youngest sister, Victoria sat next to Lady Arundel in obvious admiration. A child wouldn't look upon someone with such longing without a return of affection.

"Thank you, Arundel. I appreciate the offer. It would be nice to have more time with the repairs before moving my sisters into their bedchambers."

"Repairs?" Arundel asked.

Ashby patted Lucas on the shoulder and stepped forward. "Arundel, you know how women are about their homes. Everything must be redone when a new mistress takes ownership."

"Whatever do you mean?" Arundel wasn't fooled. An underlying annoyance at his father hid beneath every word spoken. "If you are attempting to make my wife uncomfortable for the changes upon Arundel Keep, you may keep your thoughts silent."

"The changes made upon the Keep were frivolous."

"You may take your leave from Arundel Keep and spend the remaining months in town if the changes are so offensive." Arundel turned to Lucas. "What updates are being done on Ashford Manor?"

"The manor has issues needing repair." Lucas didn't want to add to the obvious contention between Ashby and Arundel, but he was an honest man and didn't care for lies. "It has seen better days."

Arundel scoffed in disgust. "How bad is the manor?"

Before Lucas could reply, Ashby answered. "There is a reason we stopped spending time at Ashford Manor. I have given Branton more than enough money to ease the pains of a renovation."

Arundel looked away from Ashby ignoring the duke. "Is the home dangerous?"

Lucas shook his head. "We have had mishaps, nothing overly dangerous so far." His thoughts went back to the bed braking and a smile crept onto his face. "Most of the time we find it a source of laughter."

"I want to help with arranging the work and I plan to get my hands dirty upon the estate." Arundel looked to his wife. "Emma, I think Marianne would appreciate your assistance with the gardens and the inside of the house."

Lucas thought about declining the offer of help, but he had to admit the work would be far less stressful with help from family. As he thought the word family, he found it pleasing. He'd never expected help from his parents or cousins. The simple offer of service made the entire task of bringing a ruined estate back to life less burdensome.

"Thank you. The burden seems much lighter with your offer."

As Lucas rode back to Ashford Manor, he pondered upon the word "family." He'd always considered it a word to mean people forced into a unit viewed by the world as belonging together based on blood ties. It had never made much sense. Now he considered the possibility that a family was much more than people who dreaded meeting during holidays or forced together during social events. Families helped when they were needed, and they offered instead of being forced or tricked.

Sixteen

MARIANNE STOPPED SEARCHING THROUGH FABRICS AS she heard Lucas's voice in the entryway. She hoped he'd enter the morning room to see the progress she'd made since he'd left only hours before. Her cheeks flushed with the hope of pleasing her husband and the memory of their morning with the broken bed.

"My lady, are you unwell?" Mrs. Harwood touched Marianne's arm showing concern. "You look flushed."

"I am well enough." It would be terribly embarrassing for anyone to know the thoughts entering Marianne's mind. She wanted to gaze into Lucas's deep brown eyes again and kiss the dimples in his cheeks.

Lucas's voice again sounded outside the room, and Marianne found a small amount of perspiration building upon her neck. How had her husband managed to unsettle her so quickly? The words he spoke were of little consequence. It was the pleasing baritone of his voice that managed to upend her nerves. She wanted him near but realized his presence would turn her into a fool.

"The carpenter is ready to remove the flooring, if you are prepared for the dust." Mrs. Harwood's reminder pulled Marianne back to the task she'd started.

"Yes. Please proceed." Marianne held the fabrics up to eye level so she could imagine new drapery. She had to keep her mind off Lucas and the growing attraction she felt for him otherwise, she'd never finish the task of restoring Ashford Manor.

"I think they look the same." Lucas's voice sounded in her ears.

Smiling, Marianne decided not to turn and face him but to continue looking at the fabrics. It wouldn't hurt to keep him in the dark over her admiration, at least for now. "They are completely different. One is cream and the other is white."

Lucas moved to stand next to her. She turned her head forcing a glare of impatience. Narrowing her eyes, she teased. "Do not tell me you want orange curtains."

"Now you mention it, I think orange would suit this room perfectly."

"This is why you are supposed to restore the land and livelihood of the estate and not the inside of our home."

Lucas's lips twitched; she knew he was fighting a smile. "I promise to not disappoint."

Marianne turned to look her husband in the eyes. There was a hint of anguish in his voice that caused concern. "What happened at Arundel Keep?"

"I owe you an apology, my dear. You were right about Ashby."

Marianne closed her eyes in fear of Lucas's next words. She wanted to know what Ashby had done, and yet she feared the answer. "You are unharmed?"

"Are you concerned for my physical wellbeing? Marianne, do not fear, the duke did not injure me. He did admit to knowing of the state of Ashford Manor. But that is all. I hoped it had been a mistake."

Marianne looked away from him. She was disappointed in her father for his role in deceiving Lucas and she didn't want to see an accusation. She hadn't known about the ruinous state of the manor. "I do not know what to say. I am ashamed my father would be so deceitful given the agreement you had to marry me."

"You are not to blame, Marianne. I hold no ill feelings toward you."

She allowed his words to sink in before turning to see he was in earnest. Locking eyes with the man, she found her stomach fluttering as his lips turned up in an encouraging smile. "Were you able to speak with Phillip about your sisters?"

"Yes. The girls are happy at this time, and I see no reason to remove them until Ashford Manor is restored. I do think we should spend more time at Arundel Keep. It would make the transition less stressful if we are better acquainted."

"I hoped you would say this. I want to know your sisters and make certain they will be comfortable here. Lucas, I want them to feel a part of this beautiful life we are building."

Marianne stopped speaking, although she had more she wanted to say, yet feared it would cause Lucas to withdraw. He hadn't spoken much about family and a future, and she wanted to help him find comfort as well. But pushing him into accepting the life she hoped for might be too much so early in their marriage.

"Thank you for caring about my sisters." Lucas backed away and took a long look at the work she'd accomplished within the time he'd been gone. "At this rate the house will be finished within the month."

Marianne bit her fingernail. It was a nervous habit she needed to break. But if he was disappointed in the changes, she would stop the work and redo everything to his liking. Suddenly, she feared he really did like the color orange. "Do you like it?"

"By removing the dreadful worn out furnishings, you have already made the room much brighter and welcoming. I anticipate we will entertain often with a room as grand as you have in mind."

Marianne took it as a compliment. "I thank you for the kind words."

"I only hope when I have finished with the land, you will find my efforts as welcoming. For now, I am set to meet with the steward and the man he would like to hire for a gardener. Together, you and I will bring this estate back to life."

She loved his inclusion of her efforts in the statement. It brought relief and joy to know he respected her choices for the house. As Lucas departed, she watched him walk away. He wasn't the man she'd expected to marry when the season began, but she was thankful he'd been in that dingy coaching inn perfectly placed to save her from Brockhurst.

Turning back to the project she was supervising, Marianne held the fabrics up again to examine the pattern. She decided to go with the cream. It had a pattern of flowers, and she hoped to fill this room with flowers as soon as her husband was successful with revitalizing the gardens.

Seventeen

THE PICNIC WAS LADY ARUNDEL'S IDEA, which only proved to Lucas that he was right about family. There was much more to the concept of a unit of people related by blood than his parents had led him to believe. The goal was to help Lucas and Marianne associate with his sisters. He wasn't a man who cried easily, but when the invitation arrived with a letter explaining the purpose, he'd found his throat constricted at the confirmation of his place in this new family. Before his marriage, kindness and inclusion had been rare. He'd spent most of his life wishing he was part of something meaningful, and now he'd found it in a family.

Lucas worried over conversation topics and how to interact with the girls as their ages spanned ten years. Arabella, the eldest, was seventeen and would need an introduction to Society within the next season or two. Victoria was the youngest. At the age of seven, she needed a governess and tutoring to occupy her days. Navigating each sister's individual needs was overwhelming to think about, let alone organize.

As he escorted Marianne to the Keep, he noticed the wheelchair placed at the edge of the blankets. Flora was thankfully sitting amongst the group. But Lucas had neglected his duty by this sister for far too long. He needed to consult a physician over her condition. It was important for him to understand what he and Marianne should do for her.

"Are you nervous?" Marianne asked.

Lucas shook his head and then changed course and nodded. "Very much. How did you know?"

"You have never held my arm so tightly. Do not worry, Emma tells me the girls are sweet."

"What can you tell me about them?"

"Arabella is writing to a young man in America. She knows him through a friend at the finishing school. She received permission from Wymount before answering the first letter."

Lucas had been worried about organizing a first season for his sister. Now he was concerned she'd want to marry a foreigner. "Is the situation serious?"

"Emma believes they are friends at best. Nothing more."

"What else can you tell me?"

Marianne squeezed his arm to lend support. "Mary's focus is on men, especially my brother Charles. But Emma believes she will take a prince if one is available."

Lucas raised his eyebrows in surprise. "A prince?"

"Oh yes. She has societal ambitions to rival those of my father. Mary wants the wealthiest man around, which is why Charles will not do for her. He is the youngest son of a duke and will not inherit a title, but she enjoys gazing at him."

"She is shallow, like my mother?" This was a disappointment. It would've been difficult for his sisters not to take on some of the duke and duchess of Wymount's poor habits, but this was one he'd hoped they would avoid.

"She is only sixteen and has yet to fall in love. Perhaps one day she will find a suitable man."

"Do you know anything about the three younger girls?"

"Flora is a mystery. She is quiet and keeps to herself. Alice and Victoria have yet to discover all their likes and dislikes, mainly because they are kept indoors with Flora. The caretakers your parents hired chose to keep the girls together at all times."

Lucas appreciated everything Marianne had to say about his sisters. This information would lay a building block for him to understand them. "Do you think it wise to hire two governesses? One for Flora and one for the others?"

"No, I believe one governess is enough for the small school room we have at Ashford Manor. What do you think about hiring a lady's maid for the three younger? She could keep Flora company indoors, if Flora does not want to be outside with her sisters."

"Marianne, you are the finest countess in the world." He appreciated her willingness to give helpful suggestions and to make her opinions known.

"Do not say such things too loud. I have two sisters who also hold a title of countess. The competition to be best has never crossed our minds."

Quickening their pace, Lucas was still worried about the conversation and how to interact with his sisters, but he trusted Marianne would be there to guide him through the difficult parts. Lucas assisted his wife while she sat, and then he took a seat next to her on the blanket. With the bright blue sky and light wind, it was a perfect day to spend out of doors.

"Lord Branton, when are we going back to school?" Victoria's question silenced all conversation.

Lucas took a moment to decide on his response. Would she be disappointed if he didn't send her back to the boarding school? "You are my sister, Victoria. Please call me Lucas." With the formalities taken care of, Lucas looked at all his sisters before continuing. "I had hoped you would not want to go back to school. Marianne and I would like you to live at Ashford Manor with us."

Mary shook head. Defiance set in her tight lips and sturdy gaze. "Mother told us we are not to be a burden upon you. If we are at Ashford Manor, you will have to see to our daily needs. This is why the duchess arranged for us to be raised away from Lydney Hall. You must send us back, with haste."

"I do not like school," Victoria said, all lightheartedness gone from her features. "Flora, Alice, and I want to stay at Arundel Keep with Phillip and Emma. They love us."

There was that word again — love. Lucas wanted to know what it was like to be loved. He was jealous to hear his sisters knew what love was. He was an adult. He should understand the meaning of all words in the English language.

Marianne leaned forward and took Victoria's hand. "Will you give me a chance to love you?"

Victoria turned her head to look at Lady Arundel — Emma, as she'd referred to the countess. Another moment of jealousy swept through him. His sisters referred to him with his title, but to others by their Christian names. He wanted to leave the picnic and be alone with his thoughts. But he was an adult, and he'd long ago learned not to let such things affect him.

"I think it would be nice." Victoria's response was forced.

Lucas turned to Arabella. She was the eldest out of the girls and would have an opinion, he hoped. "Arabella, what of you? Would you prefer going back to the finishing school our parents dumped you in, or find a home at Ashford Manor?"

"I appreciate your offer, Lucas. It is my opinion a home at Ashford Manor will be preferable to going back to school." Before Lucas could respond, she held up a letter. "As long as I may continue to write to my friend in America. Lord Arundel has not allowed it while in his home, and I have approval from the duke."

Lucas focused his eyes on the thick letter in Arabella's hand. "I would like to know more about the situation before committing. I think you should be focused on entering Society."

"May I enter Society? If I choose to stay at Ashford Manor, will you let me enter Society in the fall?" Mary's excitement was obvious as she went up on her knees and straightened her posture. "I have dreamed about entering the royal courts for so long. Do you think the Prince Regent will be in attendance?"

"The Prince Regent might be in attendance. Why do you ask?" Lucas feared her answer. If she intended to flaunt in front of the prince, it would be disastrous. The prince was married. Lucas would need to speak to his sister about propriety.

"If he is in attendance, then Prince Adolphus might be there. And I could find someone to introduce us. Perhaps the queen would be so kind." Mary was off in a different world, if she thought one of the princes would marry outside of royalty. The suggestion of having the queen make their introduction was laughable, but only because Duke Wymount was a recluse and hadn't seen to his duty of entertaining the elite of Society for far too long.

Biting his tongue, Lucas looked to Marianne for help. He hadn't any idea how to stop the girl from expecting impossible results. Marianne leaned forward and whispered in his ear. "Let her dream, if only for a little while."

"I think it would be easier on me if only one sister was out in Society at a time. Once Arabella is settled, we will discuss your entrance."

Mary pouted and allowed her perfect posture to slump. "I would prefer going back to school. I hate Sussex and I hate Arundel Keep. Mother said you were given a sizable dowry to marry Lady Branton. You have the funds to send me back to school."

"If it is what you wish, I will arrange for you to go back."

"I prefer to go where I know no one cares about me. It is better than having a long-lost brother come into our lives and pretend he wants us around. You do not care for us."

"Mary, I have spent my life alone. Our parents sent me to school and left me to the care of servants, just as they did you. The only difference between you and I, is I did not have siblings to spend time with. You are close to our sisters. You should understand what family is, more than I do."

The picnic had taken a dangerous turn, at least in Lucas's mind. He'd hoped for laughter and lighthearted conversation. But he also understood his sisters were worried about their futures. A familiar dislike for his parents entered his soul and festered deep down as he sat back and listened to conversation between Marianne's family. As he watched their interactions, he wished more than ever, that his parents had cared for him and his sisters.

Lucas needed time to think. Instead of watching as Marianne easily became friends with his sisters, he had to leave the group and gather his thoughts. It pleased him to see her ability to speak with each of the girls, but it left him aware of the inadequate way he'd handled the questions thrown in his direction.

"If you would like to be alone, you only need tell me to leave." Arundel matched Lucas's pace, and Lucas found he didn't mind having the company.

"May I ask your advice?" When Arundel nodded, Lucas continued. "How did you win the admiration of all my sisters?"

"It is a natural gift. I have always had an easy time conversing with women."

Lucas scoffed. "You are not helping."

"You are nervous around them, and they know. Mary will take advantage if you let her. Alice and Victoria want to be loved. Arabella needs a male figure in her life to show her how to behave in Society, and Flora is waiting for someone to notice she does not need a wheelchair."

Lucas stopped walking. He'd hoped Arundel would have insight into Flora's condition, but this was much more than he'd expected. "What do you mean? Why would Flora use the chair if it isn't needed?"

"Because no one ever noticed she was well. The poor girl has been neglected for most of her life and no one paid enough attention."

"Did she confide in you?"

Arundel shook his head. "No. Emma found Flora dancing by herself in the ballroom. We did not think it our place to pry."

"Thank you for telling me."

"Branton, I fear you have a taken on more than you expected. Emma and I are here if you need us."

"I will speak to Marianne, but after today I think it is best my sisters are settled at Ashford Manor before the week is out."

"I agree. They need a home and stability."

Lucas ran a hand through his hair. He wasn't certain he knew how to provide stability. He could put a roof over their heads, food on the table, and clothing in their closets, but was it enough?

"Branton, something is bothering you. Can I help?"

Arundel had been his friend for many years. After leaving Oxford, they hadn't seen each other on a regular basis, but Lucas still considered him a trusted friend. Could he ask the question plaguing him?

Lucas regretted the question the moment he opened his mouth to speak, but he needed to understand and learn how to love. "My sisters claim you and Lady Arundel have shown them love. Will you tell me how to do the same?"

If someone had asked Lucas the same question, he would have laughed. It was a mark of Arundel's character when he took a moment to seriously consider an answer. "We have seen to their needs and shared our lives with them. We take an interest in what they are doing and even though it is frowned upon, we invite all five girls to take their meals in the dining room, when Ashby isn't visiting."

"This is what Victoria meant when she said you had shown her love?" Such simple things were within his grasp. Lucas could take an interest in everything his sisters chose to pursue. "It is so simple."

"Branton, has neither of your parents ever shown you love?"

Lucas didn't want to be pitied, but he also couldn't claim such a relationship without it being a lie. "No. My parents wanted nothing to do with me. I was raised by servants who didn't care for me, and I was educated by professors."

"Lud."

"There is no reason to pity me. Up until I discovered the state of my father's finances, I lived a life of luxury. I cannot complain as I had everything I needed."

Arundel shook his head. "No, Branton, you had your physical needs cared for, but not emotional needs."

"I cannot imagine Ashby showing love to anyone."

"No, you are correct. But my mother taught and showed her children love and acceptance. I cannot imagine having Ashby as a father without my mother."

Lucas found the green-eyed monster of jealousy waking within his stomach. If only one of his parents had taken notice of their children, his life and that of his sisters could have been completely different.

Arundel's assessment of Lucas's emotional needs had been correct. Everything he'd experienced as part of Marianne's family had been a new experience. They made him think he was welcome in their home. He didn't regret spending time in conversation, and he enjoyed this new life. Gone were the days where he sat alone in his London flat waiting for an invitation to a party and then finding himself lonely amongst the desperate mothers hoping to marry off their daughters to a titled man.

"Arundel, I know this might sound very strange and I mean no disrespect to your family, but I am very happy Brockhurst chose to abduct Marianne." He hadn't been eloquent in his statement, but when Arundel patted him on the shoulder, he knew there was understanding. If that one event hadn't happened, he would be alone at Wymount House struggling and relying upon a miracle to restore his father's estates. Instead, for the first time in his life, he knew there were people who wanted him around.

"You have not spoken a word since we left Arundel Keep." Marianne sat next to Lucas on the sofa and took hold of his hand. The simple act of touching his hand sent a pang of longing through his soul.

"Marianne, what does the word love mean to you?" He needed to understand her desire for love. She'd told him it was her greatest hope for their marriage, and yet he didn't know how to show her such affection.

"I want to serve those I love and offer companionship."

"Is it really so simple?"

"Yes."

Lucas shook his head to clear the confusion he constantly experienced when thinking about love. He didn't want Marianne to know about his childhood and the lonely hours of sitting in a classroom or holidays spent on his own because his mates had left to spend time with their families. He'd never told any of them that his parents didn't want him home for Twelfth Night, Christmas, or the summer. The times they did take him home, he was still lonely amongst the people who should have cared about him.

He looked to Marianne. "I have no problem offering you companionship. I want us to be the best of friends."

"Lucas, you are missing the underlying part of love. Love is not a friendship between husband and wife. Certainly, it is important to like each other and enjoy each other's company, but there are emotions and feelings involved."

He'd had moments where he'd desired Marianne, but deep in his soul he knew she wasn't speaking about desire. She wanted something more from him, and her simple answer from moments before didn't convey the emotions she associated with love.

"I worry I will never be able to give you what you need."

He'd injured her feelings. It was apparent from the way she looked at her hands and refused to meet his gaze. Lucas put a hand under her chin and lifted her eyes so he could see the beautiful blue and the pain his words had caused. "I want more than anything in this world to know what love is, but I find myself incapable of expressing something I have never experienced."

Marianne touched his face. She ran her hands along his jaw and when she leaned forward to give him a kiss, like the one she had the morning they'd been trapped in the broken remnants of the bed, Lucas closed his eyes to enjoy her tender lips upon his cheek. "Lucas, one day you will understand love. I promise to teach you."

His mouth went dry as his wife pulled away, the warmth of her closeness going with her. He wanted to pull her back and spend the rest of the evening talking about matters of the heart, but words escaped him. When she was no longer in the room, he looked down at the book he'd been reading about rearing sheep and started a new chapter.

Eighteen

SOMETHING WAS WRONG. MARIANNE KNEW FROM the moment Lucas exited the carriage. His jaw clenched, eyes distant, and conversation short told her he wasn't happy. She'd never seen her husband in such a state and found she didn't like his temper. Lucas stormed into the house, tripped over a new hole in the floor, and locked himself away in the den. After asking Mrs. Harwood to take him a tray with tea and cakes, she left to continue the redecorating of the music room. She didn't see Lucas again until he joined her for supper.

His mood hadn't improved, and so Marianne had a choice to make. She could allow her husband to sit in silence while picking at the food on his plate, or she could tell him about her day. The restoration project was a source of pride for her, and she hoped it would pull him out of his thoughts. "I finished the music room today. New instruments will arrive in the morning. I plan to find a governess to teach Flora, Alice, and Victoria the piano, violin, and harp."

"I have a feeling my sisters will be accomplished women when you are finished with their education."

"It will help them find husbands, when the time is right."

"Husbands? With the lack of a dowry my sisters will not have the opportunity to wed, at least not within the comforts of Society." Lucas let out a slow moan and put his head in his hands. "I hate my father for the mess he and my mother made of the estate finances. And although I refuse to give up on correcting the errors, I see no way of giving Arabella and Mary a dowry."

Marianne had considered Lucas's silence on his father's financial difficulties to mean he would never confide in her. If this was a simple slip of the tongue, she didn't know. She thought about making inquiries to show her interest but worried it would stop him from speaking further upon the subject. She wanted to share this burden with him, and the hope building within her left her waiting for the moment she could show support.

"Your discussion with the solicitor did not go well?" He'd told her he was meeting with a solicitor, but she hadn't known it was about Wymount's estates.

"He believes I can restore Wymount's estates to proper working order, but it will take seven to ten years to turn a profit."

"What of this estate? Is it as dreadful as Wymount's lands?"

Lucas shook his head. "No. Ashby kept the land profitable to support his needs. We will gain profit from this estate, but not enough to build a dowry by next season."

"Is there not enough within my dowry to place a sum upon Arabella?"

Lucas looked up from the meat and potatoes he had yet to eat. She worried over his lack of appetite. "I could not take what is rightfully yours and give it to my sister. I will work with the solicitor to find another solution."

"My dowry is for our family. It is not to be kept sitting within the coffers while your sister needs a proper match." She tried to keep her tone calm, but her husband's inability to see a simple solution was infuriating. "We also do not know how long it will take her to make a match. Wymount's estates could be restored long before the dowry needs to be paid."

"You would not despise me for settling an amount upon my sister when I have brought so little to this marriage?"

Marianne placed her fork and knife on her plate, unable to continue the pretense of eating. "I will hear no more refusals upon this subject. Arabella needs a dowry, and we are able to provide one. Make certain you do so with haste."

She'd hoped her words would bring a smile to his face, instead, his shoulders slumped further. "Marianne, I am unworthy of your generosity. You are filled with a kindness I have never known."

She found the familiar warmth of a blush rushing up her neck to land in her cheeks. Would her ability to show compassion be the key to helping him understand love? His denial of the existence of love would be a challenge to defeat, but she hoped over time he would come to understand the reason she'd insisted on a dowry for Arabella was due to her growing admiration for him. If it was love, she couldn't yet say. But the desire to be near him grew each day, and when he was in a separate room or away dealing with estate business, an ache to have him near pressed upon her heart.

"I cannot bear to see you so distraught. I want you and your sisters to be my family. Family gives and cares for one another."

"I am learning this concept. I admit it is strange to have people who care about what happens to me. I am swimming in uncharted waters."

Marianne wanted him to know of her sincerity, but she couldn't help bringing in a bit of humor. "I could arrange for another tub to break while you are bathing to help you practice swimming."

Lucas perked up with her saucy comment. A wide grin replaced the frown he'd shown since earlier in the day. It didn't erase the concern she knew he carried, but it was nice to see a livelier version of her husband. "Traitorous valet. Is there not a servant who can be trusted with such personal information? I will have to discover your secrets. Where is your lady's maid?"

Laughing as he winked in her direction, Marianne didn't mind the return of her previous blush. She wanted Lucas to know of her playfulness. "I have created alliances with all our servants. They will be loyal to me."

"I will hire a new staff. This treachery cannot go unchecked."

"It will be of no use, my lord."

"Why not?" Lucas stood and walked toward her. She knew he hadn't eaten. She would insist he take tea and nourishment once they were settled in the drawing room.

"I will win them over, as I have this staff. Your efforts will be in vain."

Lucas lifted her hand and placed a gentle kiss upon her knuckles. Butterflies fluttered in her stomach. She loved the tenderness he displayed in such moments. "I do not doubt your ability to charm a new staff. I will save you the need by acknowledging defeat."

She allowed him to escort her into the drawing room and was pleased when he took a seat next to her on the sofa. She pulled out her needlework and he entertained himself with a book on finances. It was a comfortable evening in a newly decorated room. She hoped there would be many more nights where they could sit in companionable silence.

Marianne had dreamed of evenings where she and her future husband would want to be close in proximity, but each engaged in a separate activity. As her marriage to Lucas continued, she found him to be the match of her dreams.

"Lord Arundel and Lady Arabella are here to see you, my lord." Mr. Harwood's announcement pulled Marianne out of her musings. She found the interruption to their evening a great disappointment.

"Lucas," Arabella said as she stormed through the double doors. "We need to speak."

Marianne held back a smile as Phillip gingerly crossed the threshold. A calm, yet amused, smile played upon his face.

"Could you not have waited until morning? I would have met you at Arundel Keep." When Lucas stood, the warmth of his presence left. Marianne shuddered from the sudden chill. It wasn't a cold evening, but fall was upon them.

Arabella crossed to a lone seat and threw herself upon it. She looked to Phillip, so Marianne did as well.

"Branton, Marianne, I apologize for interrupting your evening. Arabella and I have had a bit of a disagreement."

"An understatement!" Arabella cried out. The desire to hold her tongue and allow Phillip to explain quickly dissipated. Arabella jumped from her seat and crossed to Marianne. "Can you not speak sense to my brother? My heart aches to hear from Albert. If I do not write, he will think I do not care for him."

Marianne patted Arabella's hand and looked to Lucas. She didn't want to overstep her position, but since correspondence had already occurred, she wasn't certain it would work to cut them off completely.

Arabella had a legitimate argument. Poor Albert would wonder why his latest letter had gone unanswered.

Lucas took a firm stance, which Marianne quietly disapproved. "Arabella, it is improper for you to write to a man who is not your intended. Wymount never should have allowed the correspondence."

"I love Albert. Can you not understand how I feel? My heart breaks with each letter I receive asking for a response. He does not understand my delay. May I send at least one to explain your ridiculous position?"

If Arabella had made her argument without adding the part about Lucas being ridiculous, Marianne was certain her husband would have given approval. His face had softened with the explanation of Albert's concern. When she'd attacked Lucas's position and claimed him ridiculous, his sensibilities were pushed aside.

"No. It is inappropriate, and I will not allow such behavior."

Arabella looked to Marianne again. "Please speak with him. He will listen to you."

Marianne bit her bottom lip. She hoped to win Arabella's trust, but it wouldn't help to lose Lucas's at the same time. She knew her words would break any relationship she'd started building with this sister, but her marriage was still in a delicate phase. "I am afraid I cannot."

"You will not help me? Is it because Duke Ashby forced you into a marriage with my uncaring dolt of a brother?"

"I am happy with my circumstances. One day, you will understand what I am saying. Also, please do not speak so unkindly about my husband." Marianne wanted to gain the confidence of her sister but allowing her to disparage all Lucas was doing for his sisters was not fair. Lucas's earlier concerns over Arabella's dowry would go unknown by everyone except her, and she could not allow such cruelty toward a caring man.

"Arabella, we are done for tonight. Lord Arundel will escort you back to the Keep and we can speak again once you have calmed down." Lucas walked to the door, his face lacking emotion.

"You do not understand." Instead of following Lucas and Phillip to the door, Arabella threw herself on the end of the sofa and buried her head in a pillow. Her shoulders shook as her cries echoed through the silent room.

No one spoke, but they each exchanged silent pleadings of helplessness. When Marianne realized neither her husband nor brother knew what to do, she scooted closer to Arabella and rubbed her back. "Take time to calm your nerves and then perhaps you can help Lucas understand the situation."

Arabella turned her head to reveal red puffy eyes and tear stained cheeks. "Lucas will never understand. He doesn't believe in love. He is like our parents. It will not take him long to send me and my sisters back to the wretched school we were raised in." Arabella sniffed and wiped at the renewed tears streaming down her cheeks. "One day you will realize he married you for the money Duke Ashby promised. If not for the dire circumstances he was in, he would have found a wealthier family. Love is not a part of his plans, it never was. And he is now destroying my only chance at happiness."

The words stung. Marianne had feared Lucas's purpose in accepting Ashby's offer. She'd purposefully stayed in the dark regarding the full amount of her dowry and the marriage contract so she wouldn't be disappointed. But no one could deny she'd had need of a marriage, and he'd had need of money.

Everything she thought they'd built while sitting in silent comfort might have been a completely different experience for Lucas. She had daydreamt of growing old with a man she could admire and love. What did he think about while she worked on embroidery? Was he counting the minutes until he could be alone in his chambers? Did he continue this forced arrangement for the money her father allocated to Lucas's coffers?

"Arabella, we will trespass upon Branton and Marianne no longer. Return to Arundel Keep with me so you can calm down and have a civil conversation with your brother in the morning."

Marianne moved away as Arabella sat up. They locked eyes, and a sense of dread pierced Marianne's heart. Arabella truly believed the terrible words she'd spoken only moments before. Unnerved by the realization that she'd made a ninny out of herself by acting like Lady Branton, wife and countess, all while working toward a marriage of love, was embarrassing. Lucas was only in this marriage for the money, and she needed to guard her heart.

Nineteen

THE MORNING MEAL WAS UNCOMFORTABLE. LUCAS'S wife ignored him upon her entrance and proceeded to nibble at the small amount of food she'd chosen for her plate. When she finished, she left without a word. As she walked away, he squirmed in his seat. Had he done something to injure her feelings? He reviewed their last interactions, after Arabella and Arundel had left Ashford Manor. Marianne stayed in the drawing room for a short time, and then decided to turn in for the night. He hadn't done anything wrong.

As he thought over the conversation at supper, Lucas realized he'd revealed information regarding his father's estate finances. He'd purposefully kept the information from her in the hopes that she would never discover the severity of his future title and inheritance. He also didn't want her to know how much he was depending on Ashby's generosity.

Convincing himself he hadn't said too much, he'd only implied financial concerns, he brushed her mood off as uncharacteristic, and he finished his meal before leaving for the stables. Even with the overcast sky, a ride on the estate would give him time to think over his plan to restore financial security to Wymount's estates.

Lucas tried to keep his mind on Wymount. He used the trees in the distance to count off his father's estates. Lydney Hall just outside of London, Wymount House in Cardington, Summerhill near

Bath, and Branton Manor in Plymouth… and his focus turned to Marianne.

His mind wandered from the trees in the distance, and he focused on Marianne. The situation was baffling. He'd wished her a good night. Greeted her with a good morning. He'd even tried to bare his soul to her over his confusion about love. What more did the woman expect?

Shaking his head, Lucas looked back to the trees. This time instead of staying in his mind, he spoke out loud. It would be easier to focus. "If I can hire a wise steward for each estate to manage the affairs, I could bring recovery to Wymount House within three to five years instead of the projected seven to ten."

His solicitor was decidedly against hoping for such results. But a good crop and wise investments would put that one estate back in working order. Lucas smiled to himself, proud of his ability to think through the situation. He let his mind linger for only a second, which allowed it to turn back to Marianne.

"What did I do wrong?" His eyes moved past the trees to see the local village. "Is she lonely? Do I need to converse more?" It was possible he wasn't attentive in the evenings. He'd spent so many years caring only for himself, he might have forgotten to take notice of her needs. "Why would she not tell me I am acting a fool?"

Women, especially his wife, were baffling. Since his marriage, his worries had increased. He received a house in need of repair, a wife, the care of his sisters, and the worries about finances hadn't gone away. If he'd neglected Marianne, could she not give him the courtesy of asking for his time?

Lucas allowed his frustration with his wife to build as he entertained further thoughts of their marriage. She spent a lot of her time restoring the manor. Did she give him the proper attention an earl deserved? She should make certain he was happy in all facets of their life together. "I do not know why everything should fall on my shoulders. She is a countess and is in control of her own happiness. Why do I have to—"

He stopped speaking as he realized he'd gone too far. This was how marriages turned out like his parents'. Whatever he'd done wrong, he needed to figure it out and apologize. As the first drops of rain drizzled from the sky, Lucas turned the horse around and made his way back to Ashford Manor. He would never forgive himself if he ruined the possibility of a good marriage.

When he entered the house, Lucas handed his riding gloves, hat, and greatcoat to Harwood. "Where is Lady Branton?"

"In the conservatory, my lord."

Lucas nodded his thanks and made his way to the west wing. It wasn't a large conservatory, but it could be beautiful if properly restored. He thought about charging into the room and asking everyone else to leave, but as he neared the door and heard Marianne's voice and the clinging of rain on the glass roof and windows, he decided to watch from a distance.

"Mr. Hailstrom, are you certain we can restore both the gardens outdoors and the conservatory by next spring? It seems a larger task than one person can manage."

"My lady, I have two sons who will gladly assist me in this project. I plan to surprise you with the miracles I can work." Mr. Hailstrom looked around the room and touched the dried leaves of the plant in front of him. "It will take a bit of love to bring this place back to life."

"Love? Is that all?" The skepticism in Marianne's voice sent a tinge of guilt through Lucas. He now understood what he'd done wrong.

Arabella's words from the previous night rang through his head. He hadn't thought anything of them at the time, other than love was an unneeded absurdity. But did Marianne question his devotion to her? He should have corrected Arabella's statement. He might not know how to show love, but he admired Marianne and enjoyed spending time with her.

Gazing back into the conservatory, Lucas decided to leave his wife with the workers. She wouldn't appreciate the interference if he was right about the reason for her silence. He needed to understand why the word "love" was such an important part of everyone's vocabulary.

Marianne had taken great pains to restore the library, and Lucas was thankful for her ambition in making the home beautiful. He knew she considered Shakespeare to be an expert on love and although he'd read the plays and sonnets many times, he decided to try and read them from the lens of a person in search for the meaning of love.

Twenty

Marianne knew Lucas was watching her from the hallway. If he wanted to speak with her, he only need interrupt. But, since he didn't, Marianne continued her conversation with the new gardener. When she finally finished, she turned around to see he was gone. Her hopes of Lucas wanting to understand her frustrations were dashed.

Marianne wanted to chase after him and find a way to get through to his emotions, but her thoughts were taken back to the renovation as the glass roof shattered. Rain and glass fell from the ceiling causing a clatter of noise from the servants. By now the shattered remnants of the old Ashford Manor no longer phased Marianne. She took it in stride, wishing she could have shared a laugh with Lucas.

Leaving the conservatory to the workers, Marianne slowly walked through the house considering her situation. How did one find happiness in a loveless marriage? Marianne's mother had lived almost thirty years with a man who cared nothing for her. Ashby had illegitimate children with maids and heaven knew who else. Marianne didn't care to wonder how many half siblings she had roaming the English countryside.

Shuddering with the thought of half siblings, Marianne wondered if she would one day push Lucas into such a life. If she couldn't teach him love or show the admiration she had for him, would the life she hoped to build crash down around her like the conservatory roof? She couldn't live with a husband who had no laurels. She needed to help him understand what her needs were in the marriage.

It didn't take long to find Lucas, as the door to the library was open. He sat with books piled on the table and floor, one in his hand. "What are you reading?"

"Shakespeare."

This was a surprise. She knew he wasn't fond of the Bard. "I find I am speechless."

Lucas gave a small chuckle and offered her the place next to where he'd been sitting. "Marianne, I need to apologize for last night. When Arabella made comments about our marriage, I should have corrected her."

Marianne thought she'd hidden her disappointment, but he'd seen through her. Lucas was a puzzling man. He claimed to not care about love, yet she knew there were moments when he showed admiration. Especially when he looked into her eyes, or kissed her hand, or sat next to her on the sofa. They had a connection and they both needed to stop fighting it.

Gathering her thoughts, Marianne crossed the room and sat next to him. "What correction would have been appropriate?"

"Marianne, it is true that I agreed to this arrangement for the financial freedom Ashby offered. I have much to confess. I made a few statements about my father's financial situation last night, and I need you to know the truth. I did accept the marriage of convenience for the money. But I also took into consideration your future. As a gentleman, I knew the life I could offer was superior to others. I feared for your welfare and knew if I did not accept, Ashby would find a man who would. I could not leave you to such a fate, not after saving you from Brockhurst's cruelty. Yet now I find my opinion was greatly exaggerated. You desire love, and I have not the ability to show something I do not understand."

She'd hoped her words would bring a smile to his face, but this was a conversation she hadn't expected. In very few words, Lucas had given her a vulnerable piece of his soul. She knew her next words would define the rest of their marriage. Her heart raced at the prospect of ruining everything. If she misspoke or pushed too hard, everything would shatter.

Unbidden tears gathered in the corners of her eyes as she found the courage to share her thoughts. She would give him a piece of her heart and help him understand love. "Lucas, I—"

"Lord Arundel and Lord Edward." Harwood made his announcement as her brothers charged into the room. No one noticed the emotion building between Lucas and Marianne. She quickly wiped away the tears.

"Branton, I am sorry to interrupt." Phillip was drenched with rain, as was Edward.

She knew her role. While the men spoke, she would take care of her duty as hostess. "Harwood, please take Lord Arundel's and Lord Edward's greatcoats and hats to the hall. Also, send for a tea tray."

"There is no time, Marianne. Although, I do thank you." Phillip continued. "Arabella has run away."

All thoughts of arguing with her brothers melted away as she realized the severity of the situation. Rain staining her new carpets and tea were a pathetic answer to the visit. Marianne even felt a twinge of remorse for her desire to be alone with Lucas. This was important enough for the interruption.

Lucas stood with urgency. "What do you mean? Where has she gone?"

"Mary told us this morning. We've been out searching with the hope she was still on the estate, but all indications show she has left Sussex."

"What did Mary say?" Lucas threw the book of Shakespeare on the nearest table. "Did Arabella leave a letter?"

The impassioned fear exploding from her husband would have been something to celebrate, if not for the circumstances. Other than his father's finances, Lucas hadn't shown a great deal of emotion since she'd known him. He was disturbingly calm at most times. She didn't care for his frustration or anger, but this frantic need to find his sister was proof he had the ability to love another person. In a way, she realized he had unwittingly lied to her. He'd told her he was incapable of love, and yet, a man who did not love his younger sister would certainly not worry about her wellbeing.

"Harwood," Lucas yelled, "I need my horse."

Marianne walked to the front of the house with her brothers and husband. She didn't want Lucas to leave before they could finish the conversation from the library, but she understood his reasons. "Did Mary say where Arabella planned to go?"

Edward answered, as Lucas and Phillip were busy making plans. "Arabella hopes to sail for America to find Albert."

Marianne shook her head in disbelief. It was a dangerous trip to make by oneself. Arabella could fall prey to any number of evil situations without an escort. "You must find her."

To her surprise, Lucas turned toward her and took her hands. "Do not worry. We will find Arabella and when I return, we will continue our conversation."

Thankful he hadn't forgotten those few moments before her brothers charged into the library, Marianne gave him her best smile. "Thank you, Lucas. Be safe."

As Lucas and her brothers left, she wished there was some way to help in the search. She would only be in the way, especially with the rain. Instead, she stood on the top stair under the overhang from the roof and watched her husband ride away. She stayed until he was long out of sight, entertaining every word she could have said in the library, and they all seemed inadequate.

Twenty-One

MARIANNE MISSED LUCAS EVERY SECOND FROM the minute he'd chosen to leave. She understood, and would never have asked him to stay behind, but it didn't take away the longing to see him walk through the door or to hold his arm as he escorted her to supper.

"Marianne, I am so happy you chose to accept my invitation for tea. We have missed you." Emma's sincerity helped Marianne take her focus off the worries and longing for Lucas for mere seconds before the ache took her attention again.

"I am happy you sent for me. I am very lonely at Ashford right now."

It was strange how he occupied every errant thought. She'd never had such difficulties while courting during the season. Remembering Phillip's question in the carriage, the night her world had turned upside down, Marianne admitted Lucas hadn't been on her list of suitors she'd considered for a match.

She'd spent a significant amount of time cultivating friendships, which had led to courtship, and she'd hoped to make a match with Mr. King. Love was her hope and through a series of mutual appearances and short conversations, Marianne had thought Mr. King would come to find her the most handsome of his acquaintance. She'd prayed for it many times. But in the end, he'd proven to not care for her.

As she sipped her tea and smiled during the conversation, Marianne mused over the silly designs she'd had toward Mr. King. She'd planned to sit next to him at the theater, occupy his conversations at balls, and win his heart. But had he ever really had her heart? All her plans had been those of a ridiculous girl. She now understood love, as Lucas's face with his perfect dimples, occupied her thoughts.

"I do hope our husbands are able to find Arabella before she does anything dangerous." Anne looked longingly out the window as she rubbed her belly. She still had seven weeks until the baby was to arrive, but everyone knew she didn't need the added stress of an absent husband.

"Mary, is there anything else you can share with us about Arabella's plans?" Emma asked.

Marianne chose to push her longing for Lucas to the side. If they could discover information to lessen the length of the search, it would bring Lucas back.

"What would you like to know?" Mary rolled her eyes and tilted her head to the side.

Scrambling for a question, Marianne was the first to speak. "Does she have the funds to purchase passage to the states?"

"No. We haven't received pin money from Wymount for over a year. We hoped Lucas would think about reinstating a little, but he hasn't."

Marianne had a considerable amount of pin money, but she also wouldn't use it to run away. She would need to speak to Lucas about setting funds aside for the girls. Short shopping trips into town for lace and treats never hurt any young lady.

"How did she plan to purchase a ticket?"

Mary sipped her tea to avoid responding. The stall tactic was one Marianne had used on men when flirting. Being on the receiving end was irritating. No wonder she'd never found a respectable match while in London.

"Very well, I know you would never betray your sister. It is an admirable quality." Marianne looked to Emma, Anne, and Charlotte to see each of her sisters nodding their heads in agreement. If Mary wanted to tiptoe around and drag out the conversation, she and her sisters were expert at such moments. After all, they had grown up amongst the *ton*. "I do hope Arabella packed a heavy coat and extra stockings. Nights at this time of year can get dreadfully cold."

"Hypothermia can set in rather quickly. I once knew a girl who lost all her toes because she fought with her brother over the last dinner roll." Charlotte kept her face impassive as she spoke.

"Lost her toes?" Mary repeated. "Whatever do you mean?"

"It is a terrible story. I think it best we do not injure Mary's sensibilities with such tales. She will have nightmares." Emma never looked up from her embroidery as she spoke. It was a show of a woman who had practiced intrigue. "I would not want her waking at all hours unable to rest."

Anne continued rubbing her belly while looking out at the wet landscape. It had rained every day since Lucas, Edward, and Phillip had left. "Little rest is intolerable. Do you think Arabella is well rested?"

"I am sixteen years old. I can handle knowing what you mean." Mary placed her teacup on the table and glared at Charlotte.

Marianne sat back and waited for her sister to continue the tale. It wouldn't be long, she hoped, before Mary was sharing the truth of Arabella's plans. Poor Lucas, Edward, and Phillip were on a fool's errand with the misinformation Mary had provided so far.

"A dear friend of mine had to have her toes amputated for leaving the house during inclement weather—"

Marianne knew the tale well enough to allow her mind to wander. She watched as Mary was drawn into every detail from the fight Lady Rebecca and Lord Wesley had over the dinner roll to the moment the doctor announced there was no solution but to amputate. It was a story Duchess Ashby had concocted during a terrible snowstorm when Marianne had threatened to run away from home. It was useful for this situation, and perhaps one day she would tell Mary it was only a parable, but for now she hoped to learn the information Mary withheld.

"The young lady was never able to walk again. Unable to find a husband who would accept her disfigured feet, she became a burden upon her family until they were unable to care for her. She lived the rest of her short life in a sanatorium."

Mary perked up; her face contorted with fear. "A sanatorium? By amputation you mean they removed her toes?"

"Yes, to both questions," Marianne answered.

"Lucas would never allow Arabella to live in a sanatorium." Mary looked to the ground, worry upon her face. She was a strong-willed girl, but a part of her cared for all her sisters. "Lucas would protect us from harm. He is our brother and is bound to do so by the title he holds."

Mary was correct with only part of her statement. Lucas wouldn't ever consider his sisters to be burdens. She was inaccurate about the reason for his charity. He wouldn't be forced by his title. Marianne knew of members in Society who cared little for their family members, and an example in Wymount should have been enough for Mary to know her statement was incorrect. "He can only help Arabella if he knows where to find her."

Mary, distraught over the thought of her sister's toes being amputated started sharing everything. For a moment, Marianne almost allowed a smile to cross her face, but she held firm with a frown. Manipulating her husband's sisters wasn't the way to build trust and form a lasting relationship.

"Arabella is in love with Albert. They have only met through letters. He lives in the Missouri Territory on a large ranch. Arabella told him of her love for horses and Albert wrote that it was a great pity they will never meet because he cannot come to England, and she cannot sail to the states. But she plans to plead with Wymount to give her the funds and an escort to America. This way she can marry Albert and live on a ranch."

Marianne looked to her sisters. They were as interested in Mary's story, as Mary had been in Charlotte's moments before.

"Has Albert offered for Arabella?"

"No. But it is only due to the separation."

Emma placed her embroidery on her lap and cleared her throat. "Mary, I saw the letter from Albert. It had an address for New York. Is Arabella certain he lives in the Missouri Territory?"

"He has an uncle who lives in New York. When the letters arrive, he forwards them to Albert. It would be too expensive for Arabella to mail a letter to the territories." Mary reached forward and picked up her cup. Within seconds she went back to sipping her tea.

Marianne turned to her sisters. "I must send word to Lucas. If Arabella is traveling to London, it is the opposite direction they were sent." Trying to keep a tone of accusation out of her voice, Marianne turned back to the girl. "Mary, why did you tell Lucas Arabella planned to leave from Southampton?"

"I gave my sister the opportunity to find her true love. I may not be a romantic, but I do care that my sister suffered. It was not fair of Lucas to stop correspondence."

"It was necessary for her reputation. It is inappropriate for a young lady to exchange letters without an understanding."

"They do not care about such things in the states. I am certain Arabella will find her way and marry Albert before spring."

Marianne doubted Arabella would be pleased when she found Albert in New York instead of on a ranch in the Missouri Territory. She was certain the young man was telling a falsehood about his family's estate because he knew Arabella would never travel to meet him.

"Emma, do you have a servant who can take a letter to Lucas?" Marianne needed to send word to get him following Arabella's tracks. As she crossed the room to the writing desk, a sudden fear gripped her chest. Turning back to Mary, Marianne looked into the girl's eyes. "Are you telling me the truth?"

Mary smiled. "I would not dare tell a falsehood after hearing about Lady Haughton's dear friend losing her toes. I cannot imagine sharing any associations with a sister who lacked toes."

Marianne eyed the girl carefully but could see no malice in her words or posture. With the goal of sending Lucas and her brothers in the right direction, Marianne crafted the letter and hoped it would bring her husband home faster than he would if traveling in the wrong direction.

Twenty-Two

LUCAS VOWED ONLY WEEKS BEFORE NEVER to return to Lydney Hall, but he couldn't ignore the need to find his sister. If she had gone to Wymount for help, she would need him to save her from disappointment. As he stood in front of the door to Lydney Hall, he lifted his hand to knock, then dropped it without completing the task. His last time at this house had been miserable.

"Would you prefer I knock?" Edward asked. They were tired and ready for warm food and a soft bed. "I do not think the butler will answer if we continue to stand here."

Lucas again lifted his hand to take the knocker but again lost the desire and dropped it. Edward and Arundel had left the comfort of Arundel Keep helping him search for his sister; they were good men. He appreciated their help and needed to say it out loud.

"Thank you for taking this journey with me. It has been . . ." He let the statement die out because he didn't know how to voice his emotions.

Arundel reached forward and placed a hand on his shoulder. "This is what family does, Branton."

Choked up from the kindness he'd received over the weeks since marrying Marianne, Lucas turned back to the door and took the knocker in hand. It took less than a moment for the door to open.

"Lord Branton, Duke and Duchess Wymount are not at home to visitors." Mason's cheeks turned pink, an indication of the awkward situation Lucas had put him in. His parents never welcomed unbidden guests into their parlor.

"Mason, is my sister Arabella at home?"

Mason moved backward and permitted Lucas and his guests to enter. "Lady Arabella is in the parlor, my lord."

Lucas stormed through the hall and pushed open the double doors before Mason could announce his arrival. "Arabella, what the devil were you thinking? Your addled brained attempt at escaping to America to find a boy is ridiculous." He wanted to continue yelling at his sister to let her know how frightened he'd been over losing her, but the large tears flowing down her face stopped his practiced speech.

Taking a calming breath, he removed his coat, hat, and gloves and handed them to Mason who stood waiting.

"Will you not continue telling me I am a fool?" Arabella sniffed into a handkerchief and turned away so Lucas couldn't see her red cheeks.

"Mason, will you make certain my guests are cared for while I attend to Arabella?" Lucas wanted time alone with his sister and feared it at the same time. He wasn't trained on how to calm an agitated woman. But he remembered the moment Arundel had taken Marianne into his arms after her ordeal, and he hoped to be successful at calming Arabella's concerns as Arundel had been. "I apologize for my outburst."

"I deserved it. Father and mother have already told me I am a fool. I need only your confirmation for it to be true."

Lucas slowly moved toward her; his hands clenched by his side as he had no idea what to do with them. "Is that why you are crying? Or did I frighten you?"

Arabella looked up and gave a small chuckle. "You could never frighten me. You are too kind."

Taken aback by her assessment, Lucas was pleased to know his sister wasn't afraid of him. It would help him resolve the situation. "Then why are there tears running down your face?"

"This arrived only an hour ago. I admit I have made a mess of everything."

Lucas took the folded letter she held out and looked at the markings. "It is from the young man in the states?" He didn't need to ask. It was obvious by the postage, but it was something to say while he tried to piece together her display of emotions.

"You may read it. It is short and to the point."

Opening the letter, Lucas chose to keep the words silent. She'd already endured the contents.

Lady Arabella,

I regret to inform you I can no longer continue our correspondence. I am engaged to a lovely young lady of the Bostonian upper-class. I have enjoyed our discussions on horses and the Missouri Territory, but I do not see a future for us, and therefore I must end our friendship to move forward.

Sincerely,
Albert Winston III

The man was a cad. Albert Winston III didn't deserve Arabella's tears. "I am sorry, Arabella. I did not expect the situation to end this way. If I caused Mr. Winston to search for a match elsewhere, I do apologize. I should have listened to your concerns and I will do better in the future."

Arabella sniffed and wiped at the tears. "It is not your fault. There was no other way for it to end. Wymount refused to give me the funds for travel. I will never find a man to love me and help me obtain my dreams."

"You have yet to enter Society. There are enough suitors out there for you to meet and dance with." He hoped he was saying the right words. He wished Marianne were with him so she could guide him through the difficult conversation. Since she wasn't, he had to wade through on his own.

"Men in England are not the same as those in America."

He was not aware of the particular differences, other than proximity. A cad in England was as much as one in the States. "If you could help me understand, perhaps I would not feel so lost at this moment. What is different about the men in America?"

"I have read about men in Latin America and untamed territories of the States performing daring stunts on horses. Vaqueros and cowboys ride as the horses try to throw them off. Those men are strong and daring. The men in England cannot tie their own cravats or dress without a valet. If they want to ride a horse, they do so properly with a saddle and perfect posture."

Lucas tried not to take offense. He was one of those men who employed a valet and rode properly. The question on the tip of his tongue made him cringe, but he was trying to be a good brother. "So, you prefer a robust man?"

"Yes. I do not want a weak man who must purchase a trained horse. I want a man who will take part in training the horse."

"There are men in England who work in animal husbandry. We do not import trained horses from these brawny Americans. If your desire is to wed a man who works with horse breeding, I will begin the search." He hated saying words like brawny and robust, but this wasn't about his comfort. He needed to think of Arabella's needs.

"You do not understand. I want to see the vaqueros and cowboys. I want to ride an unruly horse and see what it is like to have no control over my destiny."

Lucas kept quiet as he listened to Arabella confess the aching dreams within her soul. This wasn't at all what he expected. "Where did you learn of such activities?"

"One of my friends at Mrs. Baxter's Finishing School for Well Behaved Ladies talks about the adventures her cousin, Albert, and his brothers engage in. They are in the Missouri Territory and have experienced riding these horses."

"Do they not get injured? This does not sound like an activity for well-behaved young ladies."

"I do not care about injury. I want an adventure. I want to go to the states and ride an unruly horse. If I am married to a man who lives on a ranch, it increases my opportunity to ride such an animal."

"Dearest, I am afraid I have no connections in America. It would be difficult to find the man you are hoping for. But I can make inquiries here. I will not force you into a marriage, but I will do all I can to find a man worthy of you and your dreams."

"Are you making me a promise?" It was comforting to see hope through the tears in her eyes.

Lucas took hold of her hands. "I am. I also know Marianne will do all in her power to help you find a match you will be happy with."

"Will he have muscles and be strong? I cannot abide a man who uses a walking stick and puffs his scrawny chest out while engaging in conversation over the latest fashions by Beau Brummel."

Lucas cleared his throat and held back a laugh. He wasn't fond of Beau Brummel, and his sister's lack luster attitude toward the fop made him proud. "I will make certain upon each request for courtship to assess the gentleman's strength and his lack of knowledge on fashion and connection to Mr. Brummel."

Arabella leaned forward and Lucas embraced his sister. He didn't want to congratulate himself too soon, because he knew there would be more tears as Arabella came to terms with losing her first love, but for now he'd successfully quieted her fears.

Twenty-Three

AFTERNOON TEA WITH HER MOTHER, EMMA, Charlotte, and Anne helped keep her mind off Lucas. She'd received a letter that morning informing her Arabella was safe, which was wonderful news. It stopped Marianne from imagining horrific scenes of abduction and ruin. Having experienced such events only weeks before, the information was gratifying and eased a burden she didn't want to carry. The letter from Lucas not only brought relief, but it left Marianne melancholy. Lucas needed to stay in London to sort out some of the more difficult affairs of Wymount's estate. Therefore, he would not return immediately.

Marianne was an excellent seamstress, and she could embroider handkerchiefs and linens without much thought. So, she allowed her concentration to focus on the conversation with her sisters and mother. It was easier than wallowing in sadness over her husband's absence. As Emma confided in the women, Marianne looked around to make certain Lucas's sisters were not in the room. This was a conversation for married women.

"His grace is very upset with me. I do not know how to please him and respect my husband." Emma's discomfort with Ashby grew each day the duke stayed at Arundel Keep. Marianne was thankful Ashby hadn't descended upon Ashford Manor.

Charlotte leaned forward and placed her teacup on the table. "Ashby and Phillip are the ones at war. I am sorry you are navigating through years of hostility. It is not fair."

"I knew about the strain between Phillip and Ashby before my marriage. I thought I could help Phillip. I was naive." Emma closed her eyes and gathered her wits. "I cannot blame Phillip for his concerns. He knows I want a child, but he is adamant we cannot be the ones to provide an heir." Emma wiped tears away as she spoke. "I fear Phillip will not yield and I find my mind is wholly focused on filling Arundel Keep with children."

Marianne continued to sew as she considered the situation with Emma and Phillip. Ashby's demand for the bloodline to stay pure with the eldest son and the lack of care for his heir had caused Phillip's refusal. Listening to Emma speak, it sounded like love was not always the answer to solving painful issues when dealing with trauma from the past.

Marianne had been foolish to believe love was enough to keep people happy within a marriage. There was an obvious struggle she hadn't seen between Emma and Phillip, and although she knew they loved each other, was it enough to keep their connection strong with Phillip refusing to have a child and Emma craving a baby?

Lucas and Marianne had yet to bring intimacy into their marriage. As Marianne listened to her sisters advise Emma on her relationship, Marianne wondered if she would make a good mother. She wanted children, and there were bedchambers at Ashford Manor for a future family. Would Lucas want children? With the neglect he suffered as a child, would he fear, as her eldest brother did, to pass negative habits onto future generations?

"When Ashby and I were first married, he was of the same opinion as Phillip. He did not want children." No one spoke as Duchess Ashby, their mother, shared insight into her marriage. "Your father is not an easy man to please, and we were not happy to be matched. Our fathers arranged our marriage. Ashby was in love with a maid, and he wanted nothing to do with me."

"How did you change his mind?" Emma asked.

Marianne saw a glint of mischievousness in her mother. She'd never known the duchess to be anything but proper.

"I spoke to his mistress, and I asked for advice on how to make Ashby perform his husbandly duty to provide an heir. My father-in-law would yell at me every evening and remind me of my wifely duty. I knew I had to bring at least one child, an heir into my marriage, or suffer constant humiliation."

"Was the previous duke as vicious as his grace?" Anne asked.

Her mother continued to sew and spoke without looking at the other women in the room. "Yes. This is why Phillip is frightened to bring a child into this family. He refuses to become his father. He knows Ashby learned abuse at the hand of the previous duke, and I believe Phillip's fears are legitimate."

Emma shook her head in defiance. "Phillip would never turn into Ashby. He may one day inherit the title, but he is too gentle to mistreat anyone."

"What advice did the maid give you?" Charlotte asked. "It must have worked, for you have five children."

Duchess Ashby smiled and placed her sewing to the side. She leaned forward and took her teacup in hand. "It was very simple. I needed to show Ashby I did not care about him or a future heir. I started painting each day and I spent time with charity work in the surrounding village. I updated furnishings and focused my mind on projects. When he was jealous to see I had occupied my time with everything besides him, he decided it was time to fulfill his duty."

"Do you think it will work on Phillip?"

"Yes. He will wonder why you no longer speak about children, and he will approach the topic. When he does, allow him to suggest an heir. He will when he is ready."

Marianne took her mother's advice and applied it to her current situation. If she stopped pressuring Lucas about emotions and love, was it possible he would discover the feelings for himself? She thought back to the short conversation they'd had in the library as he'd started speaking to her about love. It was a topic he worried about and had pondered over. When he came home, she would do all within her power to stay silent on the subject and allow him to bring it up.

Marianne entered the nursery at Arundel Keep. Flora, Alice, and Victoria were happily occupied with canvas and painting supplies, but she hoped to build a relationship with each of the girls. It wouldn't be long before they were living at Ashford Manor, and every attempt would make the transition easier. As she entered, all three girls greeted her with formalities. Marianne planned to put an end to such ridiculousness with haste.

"Please, call me Marianne. I am your sister. We should be the best of friends." When none of them spoke in response, Marianne moved into the room and examined their paintings. "You are all very talented."

"Thank you, Marianne." Flora sat in her wheelchair. Although her reach was limited, the canvas was placed at the perfect height for a child in a chair.

Marianne knew Phillip and Emma suspected the chair wasn't necessary, but it hadn't been confirmed. It was possible Flora could leave the chair for short periods, but needed it long term. At the age of eleven, Flora should be learning to dance and preparing for the eventuality of joining Society. In a chair, dancing wasn't an option. "Do you enjoy painting?"

"No." Alice's lips turned into a pout forcing Marianne to hold in a laugh.

"We only paint because Harriett said we have to stay together. We don't have another maid to watch us out on the grass." Victoria put her paintbrush down and turned to glare at the maid who was sitting in the corner.

"Harriett, if the girls would like to spend time out of doors, I will take them." Marianne looked around to find the closet with bonnets and shawls.

"It isn't about not wanting to go out of doors. Lady Flora cannot play as the other girls, and it isn't fair to have her watch her sisters run around all day."

Marianne understood the predicament. Making a quick decision, she looked back to the maid. "Will you please take Alice and Victoria out to the meadow. Even though it is fall, there are still wildflowers a plenty for the girls to gather. Flora and I will see what we can find in the gardens here at the Keep."

This decision would give her a chance to speak with Flora and hopefully gain the young girl's trust. With the help of a footman, Flora was carried down the stairs along with her wheelchair, Marianne hoped everything would go smooth. She made a mental note to ensure the governess and lady's maid they hired would understand the girls needed to engage in different activities. It was important for each one to develop the talents they possessed.

Marianne walked behind Flora, pushing the wheelchair on the gravel walkway. It wasn't as easy as she'd hoped, but she was determined to give Flora a wonderful afternoon out of doors. "Do you have a favorite flower?"

"I like roses. Red roses are my favorite."

Marianne knew there were many roses at Arundel Keep during the spring. But it was too late in the year for red roses to bloom. "I will ask Mr. Hailstrom to plant roses in the gardens of Ashford Manor for you to enjoy."

"I would like that." Flora quieted as Marianne talked of all the improvements she was making in the conservatory. She hoped Flora would want to spend time in that particular room. When she paused to take a breath, she was surprised by Flora's boldness.

"Can you keep a secret?"

This was not what Marianne expected. She appreciated the young girl's trust and Marianne yearned to be a confidant for all her sisters no matter their age. "You may confide in me."

"I do not have to stay in this chair. My legs work perfectly."

This was a surprise. It was also a secret she shouldn't keep. Pushing the chair to a bench, Marianne sat hoping the words she said to the young girl would help and not hinder the situation. "Is there a reason you stay in the chair?"

Flora shrugged her shoulders. "No one has ever expected me to walk, not since I was too sick. But even then, they kept me in bed."

"Why did they give you the chair?"

"I had a terrible fever when I was little, and the doctor said it affected my heart. He told Duke and Duchess Wymount I would have to be in a chair for the rest of my life and so I have used the chair since then."

Marianne now understood what her sister was saying. "You can walk, but it is dangerous for you to do so. It could cause your heart to stop working."

Flora shrugged her shoulders. "Perhaps. But I am the only one who knows for certain that my heart is healthy."

"What makes you so certain?"

Flora smiled. "When I am alone at night I like to dance."

This was a confidence Marianne was certain she couldn't keep. She would have to convince Flora it was in her best interest to forgo the chair. If Flora loved dancing, Marianne would find her a dance instructor. "Why are you confiding in me?"

"You are the first person to spend time alone with me. My sisters always complain about having to do indoor activities because I am an invalid, and so I have let them believe it is true."

The more Marianne discovered about her new family, the more discouraged she became. It should have made her heart soar to have the confidence of one of her new sisters, but instead she worried her efforts would never be enough to break the cycle of neglect. She could never erase the lack of care and love, but she had hoped to show each of her new sisters and her husband what it was like to be loved. She would continue to make every effort, but it was hard not to be overwhelmed by the daunting task.

"Flora, may I ask you to trust me?"

Flora nodded with excitement. It brought a glimmer of hope to Marianne. The young girl was aching for attention and love.

"I would like to send for a physician. I want to make certain your heart is healthy enough for you to spend your nights dancing."

The smile on Flora's face diminished. "I do not care for physicians."

"I understand, but I would like to hire a dancing tutor for you, and how can you learn to dance if you are in this chair?"

"Why would you do that? Dancing is not part of the education my mother approved for us. She told our headmistress at Mrs. Baxter's Finishing School for Well Behaved Ladies that we did not need to learn anything above the basic steps for a dance."

Marianne rested against the bench to ponder the reasons Duchess Wymount would refuse to have her daughters trained in the art of dance. It was a necessary part of every high-born lady's education.

"Did your mother not expect you to attend parties and balls?"

"No. She said when the time came father would offer men a large dowry to marry us. She did not care to take us into Society." Flora looked down at the ground. "She refused to even speak about an introduction into Society for me. She is embarrassed by my wheelchair."

"I am sorry you had to endure such pain. Trust me, Flora, even if you must stay in the wheelchair, I will plan the most amazing introduction for you. When you are eighteen."

"Eighteen? Why so late?"

Marianne knew how anxious young girls were to join Society. When she was young, she'd wanted to grow up quickly and spend her evenings dancing with fine gentlemen. She'd had many years of parties, and now she was married to a man she'd never actually danced or flirted with. "You will understand one day. For now, let us send for a physician so we can ascertain the condition of your heart."

Twenty-Four

Lucas missed Marianne more than he'd ever thought possible. Every time he entered a room, he expected to see her standing with fabric swatches ready to ask his opinion and then tease him about his choice. When he realized she wouldn't be at Lydney Hall, in any of the rooms, he desired to leave with haste for Ashford Manor.

Lucas sat by the fireplace, reading a book on crops. Arabella stitched on the sofa, Edward found diversion with a solo game of cards, and Arundel played the piano. It was the first time Lucas had found Lydney Hall peaceful. It was a different place with people who wanted to be near him.

"My lord," Mason said, interrupting Lucas's study of cereal yields from the previous century. "His grace requests your presence in his sitting room."

Lucas placed his book on the table, planning to revisit the history of wheat upon his return. He stood and was surprised when Arabella made her way to his side.

"I would like to come with you. Mason, did father ask for me?"

Mason shook his head. "I was sent for Lord Branton."

"Lucas, will you ask father if I can speak with him?"

"Is there something you need?" Lucas knew the duke would not entertain Arabella's request for an audience. Instead, Lucas would do all in his power to assist her and keep his sister out of the duke's reach.

141

"I wanted to request the amount of my dowry. If I am to enter society, I should know what he is willing to offer for me."

Lucas had already decided upon an amount. He hadn't yet settled the money on his sister, this was one reason he hadn't yet left for Sussex. He would meet with the solicitor in the morning to discuss the estate and other financial matters.

"You have a healthy dowry of five thousand pounds. There is no need to fret over the sum."

Arabella's mouth turned down. "I was not expecting such a large amount. Are you certain the estate can afford such a large sum?"

His sisters shouldn't be burdened by the financial distress of the estate. Lucas nodded and pointed her back to her chair. "Your concern is unneeded. All will be well."

As he slowly followed Mason up the marble staircase and down a long corridor of empty bedchambers, Lucas entertained possible topics of conversation which would have pulled Wymount out of his seclusion. He'd never been sent for in his entire life. Wymount wanted nothing to do with him. What had changed?

Mason tapped lightly upon the door and waited. When Wymount called out, he opened the double doors and Lucas passed through to the sitting room his parents shared.

"Your graces," Lucas said, noticing his mother lay comfortably on a sofa near the fireplace with a compress on her forehead. He dipped his head in the proper manner and nervously waited.

Wymount lowered his newspaper enough to take notice of Lucas. "When will you and your guests leave Lydney Hall?"

"I have business with a solicitor on the morrow. We will leave once all is settled."

"Estate business?"

Lucas raised his eyebrows in surprise. The last time he'd tried to discuss such matters with his father, it had been laughable. "Yes."

"I was not pleased when you went behind my back with Duke Ashby to take control of my estate. But, now that I do not have to worry about crops, tenants, and financial matters, I am happy."

Lucas closed his eyes to stop the displeasure from spreading across his face. He needed to take a moment and breathe slowly to calm his irritated thoughts. When he was ready to respond, Lucas opened his eyes and looked directly at his father. "I am happy to hear these last weeks have allowed you peace of mind."

"I am glad to hear you say as much." Wymount threw his newspaper aside and stood. Straightening his waistcoat, the duke walked to the sideboard and poured himself a drink. Lucas knew he wouldn't be offered refreshment and a small part of him resented his father for the ignorant treatment. "The duchess and I plan to attend Societal functions over the next few months, and we need a new wardrobe. You will transfer a sum large enough for all the items we need into our account before you leave town."

It wasn't a request or even a question. The duke had made a demand. But Lucas wasn't going to give in so easily. "I allotted a sum large enough to last you through the quarter. What have you done with it?"

"We had expenses," Duchess Wymount lazily admitted.

"You spent every last quid?"

Wymount shifted uncomfortably on his feet. "It was necessary to maintain our current comforts."

He hadn't yet taken any actions to close the London house, but his father's request for more money had thrown Lucas into action. By morning, everything he now said would be truth. "I wish I had the liberty to do so, your grace. Unfortunately, you and the duchess have used the yearly allowance your estate can afford. Before I leave town, I plan to arrange your transfer to Wymount House where you and the duchess will spend the next five years with a frugal allowance. There will be enough for your needs and comforts. There is no need to argue. I have already set in motion the closing of Lydney Hall."

The duchess sat up and threw her compress to the floor. "You do not have the right to control our finances and our lives."

Lucas knew he would one day meet this type of resistance, but he hadn't expect it so soon. He'd hoped his parents would have understood the dire situation of their estate and humbly accepted his efforts. "Duke Ashby spoke to Parliament. It was a quiet affair, but Wymount was shown to be incapable of running the estate. I have taken control as the heir, and this gives me the power to dictate an allowance and your lodgings."

He might have been mistaken, but he was certain he saw a sense of relief spread across Wymount's face. His father didn't argue or resist any of Lucas's actions; instead he accepted the terms of moving to the country without hesitation. If Lucas understood the expression, Wymount had been honest when he said he was at peace with the transition of authority.

He excused himself and left his parents to their solitude. As the door closed behind him, he heard the duchess yelling at the duke, but Lucas would not yield. The estate couldn't support the frivolity of London any longer.

Lucas wanted to leave London. His thoughts centered upon Marianne, which left him baffled. He missed her more than he'd ever missed anyone or anything and each day he delayed by sorting out his father's affairs and packing up Lydney Hall, he regretted the distance from his wife. The practicality of speaking with solicitors and advisors on Wymount's debts was overwhelming, but important.

With the final decisions made, and his parents' carriage bounding down the cobblestone road, he was ready to return to Sussex and Marianne. As it was his final night in London, he chose to spend it in the library searching through books to figure out love. He was left in the same situation as he had been when Marianne found him at Ashford Manor: hopeless.

"Am I interrupting?" Arundel spoke from the door, waiting for an invitation to enter. He was thankful both Arundel and Edward had chosen to stay until his business in town was finished.

"No. Please come in."

"You have had a lot on your mind lately. I hoped to lend assistance."

Lucas turned away from the window and chuckled. "I do not think anyone can help at this point. I have plans in place to restore Wymount House to its former glory, but it will take years of solid crops to do so."

"I was not speaking about the estates."

Lucas knew Arundel was perceptive, but he wasn't certain anyone could help him with his worries over love. "Then what was your quest?"

"Lucas," Arundel paused. "I hope you do not mind if I address you so informally?"

"Of course not."

"Good. Your sisters have been at Arundel Keep long enough for me to know there is a serious doubt amongst more than one of them on the attributes of love. I apologize for having heard Arabella's comments to Marianne the night before she left, but it made me realize you also hold this same misconception."

Lucas tried to play coy. He didn't want to speak of love with Arundel. "Whatever do you mean by that?"

"You do not believe that love exists."

To deny this statement would make Lucas a liar. He'd never been known to be a dishonest man, and he wasn't about to start down the path of being untrustworthy. "You have found me out. I am incapable of understanding and expressing the simplest word in the English language."

"Have you taken the time to research the term?"

Lucas threw his hands in the air. This was absurd. Certainly, he'd spent time researching love. He'd studied the dictionary, the plays of Shakespeare, the sonnets, and poetry until his mind was full of fog. It didn't take a genius to read words and find meaning. But it left him at a loss as to how anyone could see love between the lines of the written word, especially when Shakespeare had characters being murdered or meeting terrible fates. Of course, the comedies weren't as atrocious, and yet he still found nothing to describe what he expected Marianne wanted out of love.

"Yes, and I have found nothing to resemble the term."

"Perhaps you did not search the correct books. Where did you look?"

"Shakespeare. You hold the Bard in high esteem, as does Marianne. I thought if anything could tell me of love, it would be one of his works."

"I am afraid you have given Shakespeare too much credit. He is a masterful writer, but his characters lived through a lot of pain and trauma."

Lucas sat in the nearest chair and placed his head in his hands. "Then I have wasted my time here at Lydney Hall. I should have spent more time studying books on crop rotations and estate planning."

"I do not think your time has been a waste. I think you need to open your eyes and see what your actions have led you to do."

"I am too exhausted to find deeper meaning in your words. You will have to speak plainly so my poor mind can understand."

Arundel chuckled. "Love led you to search for a sister who ran away from home. It helped you calm her broken heart and allowed you to sooth her concerns. Love also helped you realize your sisters weren't going to receive the care they needed in the finishing school, so you agreed to take them into your home and care for their needs."

"It is what family does. That is all." Lucas looked down at his hands and shook his head. In truth, it was not the main reason he'd removed the girls from the finishing school. "I had another reason for removing them from school. The living expenses were astronomical."

"No one will fault you for saving on the expense, especially given Wymount's debts. But even with saving money, I happen to know a few people who would not do as much for family."

"My parents." Lucas looked at his hands clutched tightly in his lap as he considered everything Arundel had said. Was he right? Was love a simple emotion and had he already found the ability to express love even without understanding what it was?

"You doubt your ability to be a good person because of your parents, but it is not necessary. You have the ability to make different choices and you must trust yourself."

"If you truly believe this, why do you refuse Ashby's request for an heir?" Lucas was certain he had discovered a hole in Arundel's thinking. Ashby wanted grandchildren, but more importantly he wanted an heir and the comfort of knowing his legacy was secure for two more generations. It was what every titled and wealthy member of the peerage hoped.

"My situation is more complicated. I do not want to pass abuse onto another generation. I want it to end with Ashby."

Lucas understood. He didn't want to neglect his future children. "Bad habits are learned; they are not in our blood."

"You are right. Perhaps I won't turn into my father. But as long as Ashby lives, I fear what he will do to a child who is set to inherit. If he lives another ten or fifteen years, he will have a significant impact on the child's life. I cannot take such a risk."

"Moments ago, you told me I must learn to trust myself. It is great advice, and I now pass it on to you. Trust yourself to be the father you never had. A good man. A man who treats others fairly and cares about his family. I have seen you protect your younger siblings, especially the night Brockhurst abducted Marianne. You protected her from Ashby, I have no doubt you would do the same for your children." Lucas hoped he wasn't making a fool out of himself. Advising someone on love was much different than advising a person on bringing a child into the world.

Arundel chuckled. "Do not tell me you have already had enough dealings with Ashby to experience his underhandedness?"

"Ashford Manor." Lucas couldn't say anything more. He burst into a genuine laugh as he thought of the home he'd inherited through Marianne's dowry. With his thoughts on the house, he couldn't help but think about Marianne. Again, the ache in his chest told him he missed her. He missed her laugh and positive personality. He missed the way she smiled when he entered the room and the warmth of her arm through his. "I think I am in love with Marianne."

"I hoped you would realize that. Make certain you declare yourself to her and do not tell her you did so to me first."

Lucas stayed in the library long after Arundel left. It was a quiet place where he could think about Marianne and the future they would build. The morning wouldn't arrive soon enough. The ride back to Ashford Manor would be cold, long, and boring, but he would be on his way back to his wife.

Twenty-Five

ASHFORD MANOR WAS LARGE, AND TERRIBLY lonely without Lucas. Marianne solemnly walked through each room she'd redecorated, admiring her accomplishments. The rooms sat in perfect order with small trinkets and flowers from the hothouse to add a personal touch. The following year, she would be able to gather flowers from her own gardens and conservatory to bring into the house. This made her happy. She hoped Lucas would find her efforts to be enough.

Thoughts of Lucas marred the moment. She wished he was there. She understood his reasons for staying in town and knew it would prevent him from leaving again so soon, but it didn't stop the loneliness from shadowing her every thought. His father's finances were one of the biggest obstacles in their relationship, even if it wasn't discussed. Lucas spent more time planning out crop rotations and dealing with tenant issues than he did focusing on their marriage.

She shook her head and looked to the ground. What would they speak about if they didn't have Ashford Manor as a mutual obstacle? It was all they ever spoke about in detail. Certainly, they'd had moments where conversations went deeper, but their relationship was still at the surface of what it could be. Her heart sunk and her shoulders slumped as she considered the burden placed upon two people married without love.

Life would have been simpler if she'd married one of the men she'd courted. She could converse with those men. They spoke of mutual friends, balls they attended, and — suddenly Marianne realized none of the conversations she'd had with the men in London were deep and meaningful. The only commonality between them was Society. Was it her fault? Was she the reason every conversation she had stayed on the surface and never found a purpose? Was she the reason Lucas kept his distance and only kissed her hand?

It was easier not thinking about such things, especially if she wanted to be happy. Marianne knew the best medicine for her melancholy was to delve into another renovation project. Climbing the stairs to the second floor, Marianne entered the rooms she held in anticipation of future children. She hadn't allowed herself to hope too much, given Lucas's reluctance to show emotion toward her, but the bedchambers could be made over to accommodate anyone. They didn't have to be for future children.

It took less than a minute for her to find the fabric swatches and sketchbook. With a new plan formulating in her mind, Marianne entered the chamber closest to those she and Lucas used. It was large and filled with orange furnishings. The color put a smile on her face and she considered leaving it untouched until she could show it to her husband. His boisterous laugh was exactly what she wanted to hear. After looking at the furnishings, she decided she couldn't leave it. She walked to the bed, picked up one of the small pillows and carried it to Lucas's chambers. She would place it on his bed and hope it brought a smile to his face.

She'd decorated his chambers in green, so the orange wasn't a compliment, but it also didn't clash as brightly as she'd hoped. Marianne laughed as she walked back to the bedchamber she planned to redecorate. She wanted to make it masculine in the hopes she would someday provide Lucas with an heir.

Sitting in the window seat, Marianne lifted her sketchbook and drew the shape of the room. She'd done this with each chamber she'd redecorated and had found it helped with making the final decisions on placement of furniture. There was much to appreciate about the room. A Persian rug, a large bed, and an ancient wardrobe.

"I think the wardrobe should stand against the other wall." Marianne stuck the end of her graphite pen in her mouth as she considered moving the wardrobe. It wouldn't take more than two footmen to place it elsewhere. Walking across the room she admired the craftsmanship as she opened the doors. It had a large and ancient interior with deteriorated wood. "Never mind, it needs replacing." She stepped away to write her findings on the notebook but found the hem of her dress had caught on a splinter. Instead of pulling at it, Marianne bent down and gingerly removed the hem with the hope of preserving the muslin from rips.

As she stood, she heard a loud crack in the wood. She knew it would be best to leave the wardrobe since it was making such terrible noises, but her imagination ran away with her thoughts. An image of the entire wardrobe crashing to the floor would destroy the Persian rug. The tiny wood splinters would never fully come out of the carpet.

Closing the doors, Marianne hoped it would put the wardrobe back in balance so it would stay together until the footmen could remove it. She'd gone weeks without anything breaking. The last issue was in the conservatory when the rain broke through one of the panels in the glass ceiling. Holding her breath, as though it would have an impact on the wardrobe, Marianne moved her foot with an effort of tiptoeing across the room.

She scooted her foot forward as the wardrobe groaned. She'd woken the ancient wood from years of slumber, and it wasn't happy. Marianne turned back to take one last look at the intricate artwork upon the exterior, knowing if it fell apart, she might never get to see such glorious craftsmanship again. She ran her hand along the carving of flowers blooming and wished there would be a way to fix the interior.

Marianne shook her head at the silliness of keeping a ruined piece of furniture. It wasn't necessary and there weren't any emotional ties to the piece. There was so much work she needed to do on the room, it was best to get back to the task at hand. With another groan of displeasure from the wardrobe, Marianne stepped backward, but strangely found the wardrobe had followed her movement. She didn't have time to think, instead she screamed as the ancient furniture she'd admired crashed down upon her.

Twenty-Six

LUCAS TOOK HOLD OF ARABELLA'S HAND and helped her into the carriage. He, Arundel, and Edward would ride with her and allow the servants to see to the horses they'd brought. Lydney Hall would join the abandoned estates until he could restore their finances. But one day, he did hope to return, now he'd had more positive experiences within the home. He hoped over time, the neglect he'd experienced at the hands of his parents would no longer sting and he could find peace.

Sitting next to his sister, he was surprised when she put her arm through his and laid her head on his shoulder. He didn't expect such familiarity, yet found he enjoyed knowing she trusted him. He would do all he could for Arabella and the rest of his sisters.

"How long until we reach the coaching inn?" Arabella asked.

Lucas put his head back against the plush cushion in the carriage. Long trips in such a large conveyance always made him tired. "We will travel a few hours today and then give the horses a rest. We should be home by supper tomorrow."

"Do you think Marianne will want to help plan my entrance into Society?"

The carriage jerked forward, as they set off toward Sussex. Lucas straightened in his seat. "We still have a bit of time before you will go to London. It might be best to start with dinner parties at Ashford Manor."

"Dinner parties? Lucas, how am I supposed to meet a man trained in animal husbandry and unruly horses if I am sipping tea in parlors while the men are off smoking and gambling in another room?"

Looking to Arundel and Edward for help, he shook his head when he realized they feigned sleep. Lucas cleared his throat loud enough to wake the dead, but it had no effect on the two men. "Not all men spend their times in such pursuits."

"Most of them do. It is what they taught us at Mrs. Baxter's Finishing School."

"I realize this, but can we not get you settled into your chambers at Ashford Manor and a riding tutor before jumping into your debut?" Lucas lightly kicked Edward as a loud fake snore echoed through the carriage.

Arabella tugged on his arm. "I only hoped to start planning. You and Marianne can make the decision, as long as it is before I turn nineteen. How embarrassing would it be to find myself one of the oldest debutantes entering Society.

Lucas nodded; thankful Arabella had decided to back down. He wanted her to enter Society, but it needed to be done right. The upper ten thousand would notice the lack of support from their parents, and it would be an instant stain upon her debut.

They rode in silence, and Lucas again put his head against the cushion. He closed his eyes and thought of Marianne. He didn't know how to tell her he loved her, because he'd made such a fool of himself by insisting that love was not possible. But he'd missed her far too much during this trip for it not to be love. Everything he'd learned from Arundel now made sense, and he was ready to declare himself.

But did the word actually convey the depth of devotion he had for his wife? Or was it a simple term, a way of ignoring the intensity he experienced when in her presence? A smile crossed his face as he imagined pulling her into his arms and whispering the words he'd kept hidden in his heart. She needed to hear them. She deserved to know of his devotion to her.

As he drifted off to sleep, his body started forward with the carriage coming to an abrupt halt. "Lud, I had hoped to rest through most of the trip."

"Why are we stopping? Is something wrong?" Arabella peered out the window and then turned back to Lucas. "There is a man speaking with the driver."

Lucas exchanged curious glances with Arundel and Edward, but he didn't take immediate action. It was a terrible time of day to rob a coach, so there was no need for worry of a highwayman. It was most likely a rider in need of directions or offering information regarding the road they traveled. "I have no doubt we will be on our way before long."

He knew of men who would demand an explanation for stalling in their travels, but Lucas wasn't one of them. He was calm and he trusted the driver. If there was an issue he needed to take part in, the driver would let him know. Lucas patted Arabella's hand to let her know all was well. He believed himself until the door to the carriage opened.

"Lord Branton, I've an urgent message from Ashford Manor."

He recognized the man as one of the footmen from the manor. He took the outstretched parchment and opened it, hoping Marianne and the rest of his sisters were well. His initial thought was Flora had fallen ill. The wheelchair made him think of her as delicate.

The words he read didn't make any sense. Marianne was injured. Injured? How? The letter was vague and left far too much for Lucas to imagine. If they'd sent a servant to find him, it must be terrible.

"Conrad, do you know what happened? The letter does not give any details."

"Lady Branton was in one of the unused bedchambers looking to make her alterations. We don't know how the wardrobe fell on her nor do they know how long she was trapped under it. But they'd called a surgeon in as I was sent out to fetch you and Duke and Duchess Ashby. I'm supposed to take another letter to them in London. Lady Arundel said you should hurry. They're really concerned."

Lucas knew he could travel to Ashford Manor faster by horse, but he had Arabella to think of and his horse was in the hands of the servants who were to deliver it safely to Ashford Manor. After handing

Conrad coins for lodging and food, he directed the driver to take them straight through to the manor. He needed to get home.

"I am certain Marianne will be fine. Shaken up, but otherwise uninjured." Even though Edward said the words, Lucas knew it was only to soften the tension filled carriage.

"I blame Ashby." Arundel's teeth were clenched, but Lucas heard every word.

It was hard not to agree with Arundel. If Ashby had given a home that was fully functional to his daughter upon her marriage, she wouldn't have been in an unused bedchamber working on a restoration project.

His emotions went from worried, to angry, back to worried, and then settled on furious. Ashby was a lousy father with too much money and influence to benefit anyone other than himself.

The hours traveling toward Sussex were unbearable as he imagined her condition and feared losing her. He'd never told her how he adored everything about her; the way she tried to focus on the positive, and her determination to make their home a place to be comfortable and family centered. She was the reason he could love. She had brought meaning into his life. Before Marianne, he'd been a lost soul surrounded by people who cared nothing for him.

Twenty-Seven

EVERY PART OF HER BODY HURT. There were some aches that could be excused away as bruises, and others were more painful. There had to be at least one spot without pain. Marianne searched every inch of her body and deduced the tip of her nose felt fine and quite possibly the top of one ear. But she wouldn't boldly claim such if anyone asked. Searching her memory for the source of her afflictions, Marianne remembered the terrible moment when she realized the wardrobe had moved toward her. Her initial reluctance to get rid of the item was gone. It had injured her and she wanted every bit of it removed from the house at once.

Marianne opened her eyes and tried to pull herself up to a sitting position. She was surrounded by varying shades of purple, which told her she'd been moved to her own bedchamber; therefore, someone had found her after the accident. Movement was painful, but she wanted to get back to work restoring as many rooms as possible before Lucas returned. Even if she only had a plan for each room, it was better than nothing.

"Do not try to sit up." Charlotte moved over to sit on the edge of Marianne's bed. The dip of the mattress sent movement through her injured body, causing Marianne to groan. "You need to rest and heal."

"How bad is it?" Her throat was dry, which caused her voice to crack.

"You are terribly bruised. But the surgeon believes you escaped without any internal injuries. It could have been much worse. It truly is a blessing."

This was happy news and Marianne would have feigned a mini celebration if her face hadn't hurt with an attempt at a smile. Lifting her hands more than a few inches was painful as well.

Charlotte's voice cracked. "You slept an entire day and night, but you still look terribly exhausted. Do you think you can handle tea or broth?"

Marianne closed her eyes to consider the question. She would have to sit up to drink anything, and the last attempt had been painful. "Not right now."

Charlotte patted her hand and Marianne winced. If the bones in her arms weren't broken, it didn't seem fair to have so much pain. "Rest. I will be here when you wake."

Marianne closed her eyes hoping she could go back into the peaceful slumber she'd recently come out of, despite the headache piercing her temples. She thought of all her favorite things, Shakespeare, forget-me-nots, and Lucas.

"Is Marianne asleep?"

Her mind was playing tricks on her, because Lucas's voice sounded through her head as she imagined his solemn brown eyes. They were always very serious with a hint of humor when appropriate.

"She is trying to sleep. However, did you travel back so quickly?"

Marianne decided she must be dreaming, for Charlotte was speaking with Lucas. None of it made any sense, and she wondered if the headache could cause hallucinations.

"We traveled through the night. I am concerned over her condition."

Lucas's voice was near her ear, and Marianne believed if she opened her eyes, he would be standing next to her bed. She needed him to be there. Needed to know that he would sacrifice a night's sleep to race to her side. As she inched open her eyelids, the pain of a smile was worth seeing the man she'd missed and thought of every day since his departure.

"Lucas?" His name exited her mouth in a whisper as she was certain it was all a dream.

"Yes. I know you require sleep, but I could not wait another moment to see you."

She noticed the swollen bags under his eyes as he gently placed his hand on her cheek. "How did you arrive so quickly?"

"I refused to stop for more than switching out the horses. I needed to be here. Marianne, I blame myself for this injury. I never should have left you alone."

"Arabella? Is she home?"

"Yes. She is in the hall with Arundel and Edward. I will never forgive myself for leaving you so long."

Marianne hesitated to allow Lucas to continue to speak with the emotions she saw playing across his face she didn't want him to pause. Was it possible their long separation and her accident had completely unhinged his stoic mannerisms? His need to ensure her health was pleasing. But she needed to know of Arabella's current state. "Is Arabella still distressed?"

"She is concerned about you. Marianne—"

Tears formed in the corners of Lucas's eyes, and she knew this conversation couldn't happen while she was lying injured in a bed with her sister as an audience. Lucas would have to wait and she needed to distract him from this course of action.

"Lucas, I am so happy you are here. I missed you."

"I was gone far too long."

"I want you to see the changes I made to your bedchamber. I even updated the doorknob. I want to hear your reaction, since I cannot take you on a tour."

"You prefer I go see the room now, instead of speak with you?" His confusion nearly convinced her not to send him away, but when his lips twitched and he narrowed his eyes, she saw the sadness he'd shown since arriving lift a little. "Do not tell me I will be residing in a pumpkin?"

Marianne laughed, and then held her side as a stabbing pain seared through her stomach. This was the lighthearted conversation she needed from him while she lay in such a state. "You are the one who said orange is a color for decorating."

"You have made every effort to make this home comfortable. I cannot wait to see what you have done." She'd expected him to leave without delay, but when he stalled and looked upon her with concern, her heart sped up and she wondered at the lack of pain. Could his tender glances relieve her suffering?

"Hurry now. I have waited weeks to share my latest renovations with you." Marianne was thankful she was propped up by pillows so she could watch Lucas as he slowly crossed the room separating their bedchambers. She smiled as he laughed.

"What a splendid surprise." Lucas said, he carried the orange pillow with him and set it on the bed. "Where did you find this? It is positively ancient."

"It was in the bedchamber I was redecorating. Thankfully, I was able to add it to your chamber before my accident."

"I am fond of the green you used. It is calming. Marianne, I am constantly amazed by your ability to bring more than the basic of comforts to this home."

Marianne reached out hoping he would take her hand. She wanted to let him know she was thankful for his pride in her accomplishments. When Lucas sat next to her, his presence was all she needed to fall asleep.

Twenty-Eight

LUCAS QUIETLY SAT BY MARIANNE AS she slept. Her insistence on speaking about anything except his feelings was curious and disappointing. He wanted to tell her exactly what he'd discovered while in London, but as he gathered his thoughts, he realized everything he wanted to say was jumbled. It was best he spent the appropriate amount of time planning out how to declare his love for her.

Love. He never thought he could use the word with sincerity, and now every time he looked at his wife, Lucas wanted to say the word to her. Although he sat with a book on crop rotation, Lucas's mind was focused completely on his wife. It was strange how quickly he'd fallen in love with her. He'd never thought such insensibilities to be possible. He was too pragmatic.

"Lucas?" Arabella's quiet voice echoed through the bedchamber.

"Is something wrong?" Lucas's sisters refused to go back to Arundel Keep, and therefore everyone was staying at Ashford Manor. Lucas depended upon Arundel and Edward to keep everyone outside Marianne's sickroom happy and entertained.

"Duke and Duchess Ashby are here."

Lucas blamed Duke Ashby for his wife's condition. If the duke had cared about his daughter, he would have provided an updated home. As it was, Ashby blamed Marianne for the abduction and her ruined state and Ashford Manor was her punishment. Lucas was tired of the duke and his carelessness. He no longer wanted Ashby's money or his supposed familial support. Ashby was the same as Wymount when it came to family. If expectations were not met, the person, if not the heir, was no longer accepted.

"You will stay with Marianne? Keep her here?" Lucas asked as he slowly stood so he didn't disturb her slumber.

"Yes."

Marianne wasn't in any danger. She was mending, but Lucas didn't want anything to force her out of bed. As he rushed out of the room, Lucas burst into the main hall allowing all the anger he had toward Ashby and his own father, Wymount, to affect his actions. He was tired of powerful dukes interfering and changing the course of his life.

It was true he would be forever thankful for Ashby convincing him to marry Marianne. The money he'd received for her dowry was more than enough for them to live a comfortable life with everything they'd ever desire. But Lucas now realized the money had been a precursor to Ashby's games.

Wymount had done nothing to warn Lucas of Ashby's dealings. He'd been naive to think he understood the duke. Even Arundel had tried to warn Lucas, while his own father had sat back and allowed Lucas to sign a marriage agreement bound to doom him to Ashby's whims. Ashford Manor was the first indication that Ashby regarded him as less than important.

Lucas sped out of the hallway and took the stairs with a speed he'd never known possible. As a calm collected person, anger rarely ruled his actions, but he needed to defend Marianne. She could have been killed by Ashby's antics.

"Ashby!" Lucas yelled. He had no respect for a man who would put his daughter in danger. Marianne had done a lot of updates to Ashford Manor, and it was unrecognizable from what they'd received upon their marriage, but there was still much to be done. Rooms that hadn't been updated, and furniture that could still fall apart. "How dare you come into my home after what you have done."

Arundel stepped forward. "Branton, it is not worth the argument. Ashby will never understand, nor will he take responsibility."

Lucas pushed past Arundel. No amount of levelheaded thinking would stop the indignation and desire for redress of all wrongs to Marianne. "Marianne is fortunate she will live. She could have died."

Ashby threw his hat and coat at Harwood. "Do not speak to me of my daughter. If you had not left her to restore the manor on her own, she would be perfectly well."

"I am not the one who gave her a rundown home for her dowry. You knew this home was a death-trap when you offered it to me."

"What did you expect? You married a ruined woman. She is not worth a working estate."

Ashby's disparaging remarks left Lucas empty inside. Arundel had been right when he said an argument would be useless because Ashby thought himself justified in his actions. "She truly means so little to you?"

"I did all I could to set Marianne on a path to respectability. One day, when you have daughters, you will understand how it plagues the soul to see a daughter fall so far beneath her station."

Everything Lucas had noticed and brushed away since marrying Marianne now made sense. He'd ignored Marianne's warnings about her father. He'd thought Arundel was overreacting by not bringing a child into his family. He'd found Ashby's discussion of Wymount's debts and neglect to be troubling, but until this moment, he hadn't realized what it all meant.

"I own you, Branton. I paid you more than a dowry to marry my daughter and you have proven to be as useless as my own children. I should have realized this when I found you in that pathetic coaching inn. Your marriage was the perfect opportunity for me to rid myself of an underserving child and a stain on my title. Ashford Manor has long been an estate I wished to rid from my holdings."

Arundel stepped between Lucas and Ashby as Lucas took a deep breath to respond. His only response would be to let Ashby know what a despicable man he was and to ask him to leave the estate, but would Marianne be upset over the way he'd spoken to her father?

"Anger will not take back the injuries Marianne has suffered, nor will it resolve what has happened here. Ashby, you offered a dowry and Branton accepted. You cannot claim it was anything more than a marriage agreement."

"Keep out of it, Arundel." Ashby yelled pushing past his son. Lucas stood his ground, refusing to show any sign of fear, but in truth his knees were weak. Ashby was a formidable man and not prone to insubordination.

"You have backbone, Branton." Ashby stepped forward and patted Lucas on the shoulder. "You were headed to debtor's prison when I found you in that coaching inn, and I promised to keep your purse full and to pay Wymount's debtors if you took Marianne off my hands. We have both kept our commitments to this arrangement. Do not spoil it now by developing emotions."

The discussion was over, leaving Lucas ashamed. He'd never wanted anyone to know of his agreement with Ashby, especially now he had realized he was in love. "You knew I was desperate. I had no other choice."

"The art of reading people is how I have advanced in my station. Emotions will always be a deterrent, which is where you have gone wrong. You decided to care about your wife. It was a mistake."

Lucas knew falling in love with Marianne would be his greatest achievement. "I have a profound sense of pity for you Ashby. When I met you in that coaching inn, I believed my life was over. I had spent the last of my funds to secure your daughter's comfort and calm her fears. I had nothing left and no way of replacing the coins I had spent. If I couldn't straighten out my father's financial blunders, I was ready to find an heiress or set out to make money in another way. To say I was desperate is an understatement. Love was not important to me and so I accepted your offer.

"I also knew if you were desperate, you would match Marianne with any rake or scoundrel that would take your money. I told myself, I was the better choice. I never intended to love her. But now I have found my life would be far less enjoyable without Marianne. And therefore, I pity you and your inability to care for anyone other than yourself and your reputation."

Ashby clapped his hands, slowly, mocking everything Lucas had said. But it didn't matter. Lucas was happy with his choice. He had married a good woman, and he needed to declare his love to her as soon as she would allow it.

Lucas regretted everything about the quick decision he made in the coaching inn, except accepting Marianne as a wife. He should have declined the extra funds and accepted a regular dowry. But desperation had taken hold of his senses. He'd played directly into Ashby's hand, and now he was indebted. Since his argument with Ashby, Lucas had taken to the third floor. It was completely untouched from Marianne's renovations, a reminder of Ashby's dissatisfaction with his daughter.

The carpets were threadbare, there were random holes in the flooring where the wood had given out, and the furnishings were long ago destroyed. He wondered if Marianne knew the state of the upper level.

"Was the rest of the house in such a state upon your arrival?" Arundel's pronounced limp became more prominent as he navigated around a broken floorboard. It brought a smile to Lucas's mouth to see disgust on the other man's face.

"This floor is worse. The others weren't as terrible." He truly couldn't remember if this statement was accurate. He and Marianne had entered a broken home, with downtrodden souls, and had managed to make the best of both situations. "Is anything wrong?"

"I came to check on you. A first argument with Ashby can leave even the strongest of men in a state of vulnerability."

Lucas looked away from his friend, now brother. "My agreement with Ashby was shameful. I had decided your coffers had more than enough to handle my father's debts. But it never seemed right, and I regret accepting his offer." Lucas plucked up his courage and looked at Arundel. "I will make amends for all I have taken. When we were in London, I made strong investments that will yield a profit within the next two to five years. I have also started a crop rotation at three of Wymount's estates and the money will be used to replace everything."

Arundel held up a hand to stop Lucas's hurried speech. "The money is not my reason for speaking with you. I could not care less about money."

"Then why did you seek me out?"

"Lucas, you are not only a friend but you are part of this family. We may be unconventional with Ashby in charge, but even as an emotionally tattered group, I cannot allow one of my siblings to suffer due to the duke's all-powerful reach. He manipulated you, which both Edward and I knew. Marianne convinced herself Ashby was honest in his offer to you, but deep down she knows what happened."

"It was always going to be announced to everyone, the offer I took?"

Arundel nodded. "Ashby is not one for secrets unless it suits a purpose. My best guess is he discovered the speed you took as you traveled back to Ashford Manor, and he realized you had fallen into the trap his other sons had done. You had fallen in love with your wife."

"This is one reason I have never understood love. How can a man be so cruel as to use these feelings I have for Marianne against me?"

"Lucas, you may not realize it, but we all knew you would fall in love with Marianne when we found you in the coaching inn. The foundation was set. You only had to let her into your heart."

Lucas shook his head. "I know the exact moment I fell in love with her, and it was not at the inn. There was too much stress and worry for such a blissful state to occur."

"I agree, you were not in love with her then, but the stage master had set the props and all you needed to do was enter on queue."

Lucas remembered the statement he made to Marianne only weeks ago as they'd set out for Arundel Keep. We could play a role. To which his wife had responded with a cheerful reminder of Shakespeare. All the world's a stage and everyone is an actor. Lucas repeated the words now and watched as Arundel smiled in appreciation.

"It is time you step off the stage, Lucas."

"How?" Until this conversation, Lucas hadn't realized his entire life had been tiptoeing around Society and his parents in an effort to avoid being seen. He'd essentially done the same thing since marrying Marianne. Lucas had seen himself as a strong man, but he now knew it wasn't exactly true. He would start by speaking with Marianne. It was only fair to let her know what he received upon their marriage.

"Show us that Lucas Grantham does not hide away on the upper floors. You have no reason to be ashamed for accepting Ashby's offer. But you do need to get out from under his thumb. It will take time, but you will figure it out."

Lucas agreed with a quick nod. "I will replace the extra funds. It is your inheritance, not mine."

"I will not hear of it. Ashby has much more than I will ever need and when I do find the courage to bring a child into this family, I will teach him about honor and duty and hope he understands the legacy of this title is not in the wealth, but in being an honest and decent man."

Lucas was thankful for Arundel's wise council. It left him with a lot to consider, but he knew Arundel was correct about the third floor. It wasn't appropriate for the host of the manor to hide away in shame.

Twenty-Nine

As soon as she was able to move without pain, Marianne slipped out of bed and walked to the door separating her bedchamber from Lucas's. She was tired of her chamber, and already had plans to change a few of the older items she'd kept during the renovation. Although she adored the purple bed linens and the new wall hangings in her chamber, she was tired of the same view and she wanted to replace the chairs she'd kept. These chairs could be placed in another chamber.

More than her desire to change out the chairs, Marianne wanted to speak with Lucas. When she'd heard the retelling of the confrontation with Ashby, Marianne knew she needed to get out of bed and speak with her husband. Their relationship was on the cusp of everlasting love, and she didn't want to miss the opportunity of moving forward. This could be a pivotal moment in their marriage, and she wouldn't ruin it by staying in bed another minute.

It was late, and she knew everyone was likely in bed. She could hear Lucas moving around in his chambers, and so she knocked on the door and waited.

"Come in." Lucas called out.

Marianne calmed her racing heart, and twisted the doorknob before pushing through to her husband's rooms. "Lucas, I hoped we could speak."

Lucas dropped his cravat and moved away from his valet. She hadn't given him enough time to dress for bed, which made her a bit more comfortable. "Marianne, what are you doing?"

"I cannot wait until morning to have this discussion. Are you very angry with me for coming to you?"

Lucas smiled and took her hands slowly leading her to the chairs by the fire. Marianne had replaced the previous broken chairs with comfortable green overstuffed seats. To her surprise and pleasure, the orange pillow she'd placed on his bed now sat on one of the chairs. This eased her nerves and put a smile on her face. Marianne waited until the valet had left the room before she looked to her husband.

"I heard about your confrontation with Ashby. I am sorry my father is a difficult man to speak to."

She loved the way Lucas paid attention to her. He actively listened to everything she said, and showed he understood by nodding and finding ways to comfort her worries. "Dearest, I might not have realized how intolerable your father could be, but I now know I should have listened to you. I am sorry for doubting your advice. I have no doubt you heard of the offer Ashby made in the coaching inn, and I owe you an apology."

"No, my love, you do not. I will forever be thankful you accepted Ashby's offer. You rightfully knew he would match me with the first offer he received. I am thankful, he chose to start with you." Marianne wiped the tears from her eyes as she expressed her feelings. She needed Lucas to know he was her match, but it couldn't be one sided. Gathering her courage, Marianne approached the conversation she'd pondered over since the day he'd been reading Shakespeare in the library. "Lucas, we never finished speaking about the meaning of love."

She watched as his head dropped and he focused on the ground. She wanted to touch his face and smooth the lines of worry around his eyes. But she waited, fearing any movement would break the tender moment. When Lucas finally looked back at her, she had to lean forward to hear. "I have so much I want to say, and I find myself at a loss for words."

Marianne wanted to rush the conversation. She'd spent a lot of time formulating perfect sentences filled with thoughts about their future. She wanted children and she hoped to raise them at Ashford Manor, but this was all second to the hope that Lucas would one day understand the term love.

"You have blessed our lives with the work here at Ashford Manor. I cannot thank you enough for the beautiful home you have built."

This wasn't the way Marianne expected the conversation to go, but she waited, hoping Lucas would touch upon the longing within her soul. "I wanted to have the renovation finished upon your return. I will continue to work on it."

"No, my dear, we will finish it together. I never should have left you to this work. I did not see it as dangerous, and I could have lost you. I pray to never make such a terrible mistake again. My life would never be whole if I lost you."

"You do not regret marrying me?" This fear had been pressing upon her shoulders from the moment she'd agreed to the match.

"I have never once regretted my decision to marry you."

He hadn't said the words, "I love you," but this statement was close enough. She was certain it wouldn't be long before he understood the reason he had no regrets was due to love. But she wouldn't force the term upon him. When he was ready, she'd accept his declaration.

"Dearest, when I was very little, I noticed there was something different about my family. When I watched my cousins and friends, I could see they spent quality time with their parents. So, I asked my nurse maid why my parents preferred to keep me in the nursery when all the other children had an afternoon with their parents."

Marianne gave a short nod of her head to let him know she was paying attention to his story. What it had to do with their marriage, she wasn't certain, but it was important for him to share, and she wanted to know everything about him.

"I now realize it was a terrible and unfair question to ask a servant. How was she supposed to tell me I was fated to a life of neglect? My parents thought of children as their duty. My father needed an heir and since he was a second son, his eldest brother having died at the age of two, he understood the need for a spare. Unfortunately, he only had daughters after me."

"No child should ever experience neglect. I am sorry it happened to you. Lucas, I wish I could take the pain you experienced away."

"There is no need, my dear." He caressed her face before continuing to speak. "I learned to take my place in the family, for that was all I was needed to do. When I was old enough the duke hired tutors to train me on the intricacies of running an estate; he made certain I was well educated. Never once did Duke Wymount tell me I made him proud or that he wanted me around when I didn't serve a purpose and neither did Duchess Wymount. My parents preferred I stayed out of sight."

She stayed silent as he took a moment to process what he was revealing. It had to be difficult sharing such intimate details. Vulnerability wasn't easy, and this confession left her with the desire to calm every emotional wound inflicted upon her husband from the time of his birth.

"My parents never said the words 'I love you.' I have spent my entire life wondering what people meant when they used such a phrase. I have often contemplated how one word, love, can be the difference between a smile or a frown, and yet it has caused me more distress than any other word in the English language."

Tears trickled down her face as Lucas spoke. She knew this was a pivotal moment in their relationship. If he told her he could never love her, she would find a way to live in a cordial marriage. It went against everything she'd longed for, but it was the life she'd been dealt.

"The word love, according to the dictionary is to admire, enjoy, approve, affect, covet, relish, crave, and desire. I memorized it long ago. I have determined all those words cannot mean the same, for to covet is a sin. Relish and crave are very unflattering words if one hopes to court a lady."

Marianne whispered, hoping not to break the spell he'd cast upon the room. "There are many ways to love."

"If you ask me, do I admire you. Yes, I do very much. Marianne, I admire everything you have done to make Ashford Manor a home. I admire the flower arrangements you have placed around the house, and I admire your patience with the staff and with me. I enjoy being near you and I delight in your company. I desire your happiness and you have a profound affect upon my soul."

Marianne leaned into him. She had so many expectations for this moment. "I admit, I had once hoped a man would tell me these things while riding in Hyde Park or reading Shakespeare under a blossoming tree."

Lucas's lips twitched, and his somber mood changed to a smile. "I have spent part of my time away from you studying the works of Shakespeare. And although we are not sitting under a spring bloom, I do want to share my thoughts with you."

"I would love nothing more."

"Shakespeare uses euphemisms to speak of love. To him, love has never been two-dimensional. In 'As You Like It,' if we are to believe his words, we would find love is based on social classes. In Romeo and Juliet, we would find love to be based upon duty or romance. But does romantic love have to be so heart-rendering as to force young couples into the pathetic end shown by those two young lovers?"

Marianne gave a little shake of her head and sniffed. She ignored the pain as it had no place in her thoughts while Lucas was declaring himself. She'd never noticed the observations of love within the works. She'd always considered Romeo and Juliet to be the height of a glorious romance.

"If I told you Ashford Manor has come to life with your presence, would it be similar to the lines in Sonnet 114 comparing love to a summer's day?"

Marianne couldn't stop herself from asking the question, and truthfully, she didn't want to. "You led me to believe you did not care for Shakespeare, yet you have spent a great deal of time pondering his words."

"I do not like him. And the reason is, I cannot comprehend how so many of his characters meet such terrible fates. Could he not have changed the story a small amount to make everything end happily? What is love if you have to kill or die to prove it exists?"

Marianne couldn't stop smiling for the joy his words brought to her heart. She had to say one more thing, before she allowed him to continue. It wasn't anything close to the long explanation Lucas had given, but it was the only response she considered appropriate. "Lucas Grantham, I do believe you are a romantic."

Lucas placed a kiss on her forehead. "Marianne, I think the dictionary missed two of the most vital indicators of love. For without these two attributes, I would still be lost on understanding the term."

"Oh, what are they? Should we write to the publisher?"

Lucas's laugh sounded through the bedchamber and made Marianne's head swim with happiness. What more could he say to show his love?

"I missed you every moment we were separated. You filled my every thought and gave me purpose in all I did. When I found out you had been injured, my heart nearly stopped beating. I could not rest until I knew you would heal. Therefore, I do believe the publisher of the dictionary needs to add 'concern' and 'to miss' to the definition."

"I missed you as well."

Lucas leaned forward and bestowed a light kiss on Marianne's lips. "I love you, Marianne. I have since the moment you tripped on the broken stair and chose to laugh instead of complain. It was in that moment I realized I had been missing something in this life, and you fulfilled it by showing me I was missing part of my heart."

"Are you in earnest?" She wanted to make certain the words would never be taken back.

"My dear, your very presence takes my breath away." Lucas gingerly kissed the side of her lips. He took his time touching her face while whispering words of love. It was everything Marianne had wanted as she'd long ago prepared to enter Society. Her heart leapt with joy as he pressed a more lasting kiss to her lips, deepening the connection between them. Although Marianne had never been kissed, she needed him to know she wanted the kiss to last, and so she wrapped her injured arms around him and kissed him back.

Epilogue

Lucas held tightly to the letter sent by Duke and Duchess Wymount offering their regrets and well wishes for Arabella's introduction into Society. Marianne stood next to him, her arms pulling him into an embrace. The evening was perfect, except for the disappointment he would give his sister. She didn't deserve the neglect. None of his sisters did, but it was their life. It was difficult to accept for himself, but when he saw the ongoing anguish and pain the neglect held over the girls, it was heartbreaking.

"I heard a letter arrived, is it from Wymount?" Arabella rushed into the library a vision in white muslin. Lucas knew Marianne had taken great care in helping Arabella select a gown, hair style, and slippers for the occasion. Without Marianne, this night would be a complete disaster.

He exchanged a quiet glance with his wife. He wanted her to make the decision for him. He could hide the letter. Lie to his sister and tell her the duke and duchess were delayed at a coaching inn. Perhaps he could pretend there was a broken axle on the carriage and the delay was out of their parents' control. As he looked into his Marianne's eyes hoping she would give him a silent answer, he understood the sorrow she expressed and he knew fabricating a story would only serve to cause greater pain in the end, especially if Arabella found out about his deception.

"I am afraid they are not coming." It was all he could say as his voice broke. Arabella had personally written their parents pleading for them to attend her party. "And I am sad to say they do not have a valid excuse."

Arabella nodded her acceptance, and with a strength he hadn't expected, she straightened her shoulders and held out her hand for the letter. "I would like to see what they wrote."

Lucas agreed, hoping all the effort she'd put into her night wouldn't crash down around her when she read the words in their mother's penmanship. *Negotiate a settlement with the wealthiest man at the party and get her out of your house. It has almost been a year since you accepted the expense of those girls. Arabella is an unneeded burden upon your finances. Your father and I could use a larger allowance.*

Arabella sniffed and wiped tears away as they fell upon her pink cheeks. Lucas handed her a handkerchief and Marianne reached out to pull Arabella into her embrace.

Lucas cleared his throat, trying to sound wholly unaffected by his parents' callous behavior. But it didn't work. His voice cracked. "Do not believe a word of that letter. Marianne and I love having you in our home."

"It was wrong of me to expect them to travel so far for my introduction. If they were still in London, it would have made more sense. But Bedfordshire is so far away. Perhaps, when we are in London they will visit."

It was easier to pretend distance was the reason, so Lucas didn't correct his sister's statement. He watched as Marianne kissed Arabella on the forehead and said the words caught in his throat. "It is a mistake on their part, but they will always be welcome to visit."

"When I am married, I will love my children as you have both loved me and our sisters."

Lucas held his hand out for the letter. "I will throw it in the fire. It is not worth keeping."

Arabella carefully folded the paper. "No, I would prefer to keep it. If I ever behave as our parents, will you remind me of this moment? Remind me that I was brave and instead of cursing the heavens for giving us such loathsome parents, I put a smile on my face and walked into the hall to greet our guests as a lady."

"I will."

Arabella slipped the letter into the belt at her waist. "A talisman to remind me of what I do not want to become."

"Is it not better to look for someone who will treat you with respect and love instead of carrying a constant reminder of neglect?"

"No, Lucas, for it is due to the neglect of our parents I am standing at Ashford Manor dressed like a princess in search of a handsome husband."

Lucas hoped Arabella wouldn't be disappointed when she received her introduction. He'd followed through with his promise and had spent months making connections with men who had an interest in animal husbandry and a fortune. He'd found most of the men Arabella might want a connection with were younger sons of earls and barons, and he was perfectly happy matching his sister with one of them, but he worried they wouldn't fit the idea she had of a muscular man. He feared his sister had built up an image of the young man she'd once fancied in America that no living soul could match, especially the pampered son of the British gentry.

"Arabella, you are welcome to stay with Marianne and me for as long as you need. You will always be welcome."

"Thank you, but we must go out to greet our guests. I am certain my future lies in the ballroom of Ashford Manor."

Lucas bit his bottom lip in concern and forced the warning he wanted to give her to the back of his mind. There was no reason to give her another disappointment for the evening, and if he took an honest inventory of the guests, he'd already chosen the man he wanted her to marry. He just needed Mr. Hensley and Arabella to realize they were a match.

As he greeted their guests, his wife standing comfortably next to him, Lucas thought about their future. He imagined they would have sons and daughters to fill Ashford Manor and when they would one day move to Wymount House they could add a few more to the family. He planned to teach them everything he knew about horses, Society, Eton, Oxford; but most importantly he knew Ashford Manor would be filled with love.

About the Author

ANGELA JOHNSON HAS A LOVE FOR the written word and the adventures one can take while reading. She loves to travel, read, write, and spend time with her family. She adores her nieces and nephews and loves spending time with them.

A native of Utah, Angela loves the mountains. She believes snow is meant for romantic moments as it lightly falls and melts before it hits the road. Angela believes through reading a person can experience an eternity of adventures.

Find out more about Angela Johnson and join her newsletter at www.angelajohnsonauthor.org.

Scan to visit

www.angelajohnsonauthor.org

You've dreamed of accomplishing your publishing goal for ages—holding *that* book in your hands. We want to partner with you in bringing this dream to light.

Whether you're an aspiring author looking to publish your first book or a seasoned author who's been published before, we want to hear from you. Please submit your manuscript to:

CEDARFORT.SUBMITTABLE.COM/SUBMIT

CEDAR FORT
Publishing & Media

CEDAR FORT IS CURRENTLY PUBLISHING BOOKS IN THE FOLLOWING GENRES:

- **LDS Nonfiction**
- **General Nonfiction**
- **Cookbooks**
- **Children's**
- **Biographies**
- **Self-Help**
- **Comic & Activity books**
- **Children's books with customizable characters**